A Piece of the Town
by Mattison M. Casaus

© Copyright 2024 Mattison M. Casaus

ISBN 979-8-88824-373-2

Published by

 köehlerbooks™

3705 Shore Drive
Virginia Beach, VA 23455
800-435-4811
www.koehlerbooks.com

A PIECE OF THE TOWN

Mattison M. Casaus

VIRGINIA BEACH
CAPE CHARLES

PRELUDE

With a sturdy handshake, they made a deal and agreed to only one condition. Henry Hernandez pleaded with Bernard Jr. just a few minutes before on the footsteps of Soto Saloon. Around seven at night, the bar was dead, but Henry felt safer speaking freely outside.

"Thanks for meeting me."

"What's this all about? I have to get home to my wife soon," asked Bernard Jr.

Henry adjusted his three-piece suit and stood tall, much taller than Bernard Jr. He took another look around in case anyone was walking past them.

"You see, *compadre*, we have known each other for a long time now."

Bernard Jr., whom everyone in town refers to as Beto because Bernie never sounded right as a kid, squished his peppered eyebrows together. He realized he had only met the man one month ago at a town carnival.

"Well, I feel like I have known you forever, which is why I need your help. Beto, you are a popular man in this town, seeing as you and your *familia* owned most of it, so I am looking for your support."

Beto realized just then what this meeting was all about. Henry Hernandez needed money. Not just any money—a lot of it. It was at the town carnival that Henry announced that he was running for sheriff of Bernalillo, New Mexico. Since the town is small and nobody had ever heard of a Henry Hernandez, it would be hard to win, especially since he came from northern New Mexico.

Henry cleared his throat and rested his hand on Beto's shoulder.

"Let's just cut to the chase," Beto said as he brushed Henry's hand off like a bug that fell on his shoulder. "How much do you want?"

"Just a couple hundred, as a loan, of course, but I also need you. I need your influence. Everyone knows you, everyone trusts you, and most importantly, everyone likes you."

Beto felt flattered, but he didn't know how true that was. He was sure that if Henry knew his family history, he wouldn't be saying that. Before he could ask the important question—"Why should I vote for you?"—he realized something even more crucial. This realization came quickly, almost like a flicker of a candle's flame, and put a wide smile on his face—the same smile he gets when he sees his children and his grandchildren. Although his sister, Denny, and he owned that very bar, he never got involved in the town's politics. At that moment, he found his way to something greater, something that meant more than gold to him. He knew that Henry Hernandez was his way to finally getting back what was rightfully his.

"Henry, I will give you the money and my support. Hell, I'll even put your face on my bar menu . . . if you do one thing for me once you are elected."

Henry flashed a look, both confused and intrigued. "Sure, anything, but how can you be so sure I'll win?"

"With my help and the things I know about this town, you will definitely win. I only need a promise from you."

"*Si, cualquier.*"

Beto's smile got wider as he realized that this would all work out. Henry Hernandez knew nothing of this town or Beto's family history. He was the perfect guy for this job.

"If you are elected, you will have clearance to items that have been confiscated over the years. I need something back that was mine. A silver Colt 45 revolver with a wooden handle and the initials G.S. on the side. You promise to give me this back, and I will do whatever I can to get you elected. After all, we are compadres, *si?*"

Henry smiled and shook Beto's hand. "*Si*, Beto, I promise I will get it back for you. Just one thing. Why do you need it back so badly?"

With a straight face, as if he was not talking to a future sheriff, Beto said, "I need to shoot someone."

CHAPTER ONE

After Henry walked away, both scared and confused, Beto looked down the main street of Bernalillo and then closed his eyes, wishing his memory was as good as it used to be.

PART ONE

It was midday 1934, and Main Street Bernalillo looked a lot smaller and a lot less crowded. Instead of rows of cars, there were very few cars, horses tied onto posts, and bicycles lying beside buildings. There, Beto stood outside of the saloon, only three years old, holding on to a few of his dad's fingers. On the other side of him stood his uncle George. His dad and George looked so similar, only George was a few years younger and about five inches taller. They both had dark brown skin and kind smiles that they shared with everyone in town.

"Well, I guess it is ours now?" said Bernard.

George took a step back. "I still can't believe Dad is giving it to us."

"Not just the bar. He said the store and the orchards are now under our care."

Beto started to play with rocks on the sidewalk. He was young, but he could tell his dad and uncle were very happy. Giddy, even. Little did he know, this was one of the happiest days of their lives. Beto followed the two brothers inside and sat at a booth in the bar. Bernard reached into his suit pocket and handed his son a wooden toy car to play with as he made plans with George about their new jobs. Both men have worked their whole lives in this bar, but it would be the start of a new life running three properties.

"Let me guess. Is this excitement because the old man decided to retire?" asked a familiar voice from two booths over.

"Ruben ¿*Cómo estás, amigo?*" asked George.

"*Bien, bien,*" Ruben Valdez said as he walked to give a handshake and a hug to George.

"When did you get back in town?"

"Just a few days ago. What's it been? Two years?"

George laughed. It had been a while since he had seen his best friend. Ruben went to work in California for some welding gig and left everything behind. Ruben reached out for a handshake from Bernard, but Bernard quickly turned his back and pretended to fix his suspenders under his suit.

"Well, it was good seeing you. Catch up tonight? My mom is cooking," George asked.

"Mrs. Soto's cooking? I wouldn't miss it."

After Ruben walked back to his booth, Bernard glared at George. "Why would you do that? No one trusts him."

"Oh, you have got to get over that. We were kids."

"He's a thief. *Ladrón sucio.*" Bernard huffed.

"It was one bottle."

"Yeah, out of this very bar. I don't know why we even let him back in here."

"Because he's my friend. Been my friend ever since grade school. And he apologized to Dad. Everything is fine."

What stopped the conversation was the band in the corner of the bar. One member started strumming the cello while the lead singer practiced scales with her voice. Beto quickly covered his ears. Once she started singing, the bar always became crowded, so the brothers decided to discuss more details later.

"Will I see you at dinner tonight?"

"No, I'm sure Susan's already got something cooking, and besides, this has been the longest he's been away from his mom," Bernard said while looking down at his son.

Bernard and Beto started to walk away. They both turned back. With a worried look, Bernard said, "Hey, George, just remember."

"Family comes first," George said with a nod. That was a saying they held in their family and passed onto many more generations after them.

George said goodbye and raced to the end of Main Street, took a left around his newly owned grocery store, and then hung a right before he ended up in front of Elburn Factory. He looked through the window and found an assembly line of women placing lids on metal cans. In such a perfect rhythm, cans were being twisted closed and packaged in record speed. A horn blew from the ceiling, and each woman stood up, cleaned up their area, and left for a lunch break, looking tired and bored.

Minnie, a shorter, light-haired, and freckle-faced girl, grabbed her bag and walked out of the factory doors. She turned a corner down the street, and a hand wrapped around her arm and then pushed her against the wall.

"What on earth do you think you're doing, George? You scared me half to death."

"Marry me?"

"What?"

"Marry me?"

"What are you talking about? You're going mad."

"Marry me?"

"George Soto, stop saying that right now. What has gotten into you?"

"The most amazing thing happened today. Something that we always knew was coming. Something that can get you out of this crummy factory."

Minnie looked puzzled, especially since she had only been seeing George for a few months now, and they never completely discussed marriage. She couldn't understand why he would ask so soon—and not even down on one knee. George told her about the good news and his new co-ownership. She gave him a hug and said congratulations.

"So, I want to marry you, and you want to marry me. I know it. All I need is a yes."

"No."

"What? What do you mean *no*?"

"I mean no," Minnie said with a straight face. "I will not marry you until I get a real proposal. For heaven's sake, George, we're standing next to a dumpster."

George looked at the overfilled dumpster and noticed the rancid smell. "Okay, you're right. I'm sorry. I just got so excited for us, and I realized I could have everything I ever wanted. How about tonight?"

"What's tonight?"

"I'll propose to you better tonight."

"You are going about this all wrong. It must be a surprise, and what about the ring? I mean, I know it's a new tradition, but Caroline from work got a small silver band for her engagement."

"Oh, yeah, ring! I can do that!"

Minnie laughed at his excitement. She pulled her headband off her head, revealing some sweat and even more freckles splattered on her cheeks.

"Can you still come over tonight? Ruben is in town. The guy I told you so much about."

"I'm sorry. We work till after dark. I'd love to meet him, but—" She sighed.

George understood. Minnie had to work in the factory because she was supporting her family. Her dad died in the war, and her mom has been sick ever since. It would be fine, except he knew how unfairly they were paid. The damn economy was cutting everyone short. George tried to find her a better-paying job at the grocery store, but everything was taken.

"I know, but guess what?" George placed his hand under her chin and kissed her forehead. "You won't have to work here for much longer."

"That'll be swell!"

George's mom placed a large plate of tortillas on the table.

"These look great, Mrs. Soto. Thanks for having me over."

"Sure, Ruben, I'm glad you are back in town. It seems like our George has been missing his friend."

Mr. Soto said, "No, I don't believe that. Not with that new girl he's been seeing."

Mr. Soto was quiet all evening, with squinted eyes and his guard held up high.

"You have a *novia*?" Ruben gave George a nudge.

"We'll talk about it later." George blushed.

They each politely passed around the plates and started serving themselves a spoonful of each food. Every person had a full plate of rice and beans with multiple tamales stacked on top. It became quiet, with only slight sounds of chewing. Ruben, as usual, broke the silence. "Mr. Soto, congratulations on your retirement. I heard the good news."

"News travels fast, I see." George's dad glared at him as if he should have kept it a secret, but George didn't understand why. Everyone in town would know the next day when they saw him wearing his new suit, which was much nicer and tailored to fit his body, much better than his hand-me-down suits. If that didn't give it away, then Bernard would have been no longer behind the bar at Soto Saloon but in the office instead.

"Well, if you ever need any help, Georgie, you know where I am," Ruben offered.

"I think he can handle it," Mr. Soto snapped. "By the way, why are you back in town? Didn't work out in California?"

"No, *señor*, it's not that. I just missed my family. If you remember, I am close with my parents, and they needed me back here just as bad as I wanted to be back."

There was a long pause from every side of the table. For some reason, no one was buying his story, not even George. Ever since they were kids, Ruben had been talking about leaving this small town for a bigger city, much bigger, like Los Angeles.

"Please stay for a little longer?" Mrs. Soto asked as Ruben helped clean the dessert dishes off the table.

"Yeah, we can have a cold one on the patio before you leave?"

"Sure, why not? Thanks, George."

The two men walked out of the house and onto the patio. Looking out, they could see the farm that George's parents lived on. It was small, with a few sheep and goats grazing in the field. The moon and stars from the summer night gave just enough light to see each other's faces.

"So, *amigo*, tell me. Who is this girl?"

George grinned. "Her name is Minnie, and she is just great."

"That's it? That's all I get? *Great?*"

"She's really great. She's got short blond hair, and it's even shorter when she pins it up for work, and she's got these light blue eyes."

"Oh, a *gringa*. Where does she work?"

"Canning factory. She hates it, but she's doing it for her family. I promised her one day I would get her out of there."

"Well, it looks like that day might be soon. You and your brother are gonna own every piece of this town." Ruben sipped his beer. "You are the lucky ones."

"Not every piece, but what about you? What's the real reason you came back?"

"There has to be a reason?" Ruben asked with a slight chuckle. He brushed his hand over the back of his neck.

"Of course there does. You hate it here."

Ruben took another sip. This one was longer and slower. He looked like he was contemplating something. His eyes glazed over as he said, "Do you remember being on the park playground when we were kids? It was always just you and me against the Olden brothers."

"Yeah, those guys were bullies."

Ruben stood up, looking ready to leave, and placed his empty bottle on the table between them. He walked off the patio and hopped onto his bicycle. Before he started peddling, he said, "There are bullies in California too. They will hunt you down, no matter what." George stood in the same position, pondering what lead Ruben to say that. He stared until Ruben turned left and rode down Main Street.

CHAPTER TWO

As Bernard entered his dad's office, he saw four messed up stacks of paper, a dusty old chair, and a few pencils spread everywhere on the desk. It did not surprise him that the office wasn't clean. This is how his dad liked to work. Bernard, on the other hand, quickly started filing papers and cleaning the dust off the chair before even thinking about working. He found his dad's coffee mug under a pile of crumpled papers and placed each pencil inside. After everything was put in its place, Bernard could finally see the wooden desk hidden under all the mess.

Bernard thought of his first official duty as part bar owner, and he remembered what his dad told his brother and him during the conversation they had about him getting too old and leaving the properties to his boys. He said the first thing to do would be to change the combination on the safe and only share the combination with each other. Bernard remembered when his dad owned the properties; not even he knew the combination. He finally learned what it was just days before but only now realized it was because he needed to change the code. He often wondered if the safe was real. It was one topic never brought up in family conversations. So, when his dad told him the location, he knew the rumors were true. Everyone knew the town liked to discuss their family business. He often heard that the money from the businesses was locked in the bank, under one of the beds at home, or buried out in the desert—that was his favorite. The one that most people went with was in the bar, and it turns out they were right.

Bernard shut and locked his office door, then pulled down the shade on the window. He walked over to a painting of the Rio Grande, lifted it, and placed it on the floor. Behind the painting was a safe with a large dial on it. Bernard twisted in the old combination. With each click that the dial made, anticipation hit him. When he opened the safe, in front of him sat about ten bars of gold, thirteen silver bars, a couple of rare coins, and close to twenty stacks of cash. Bernard blinked in disbelief. He figured his dad hid money in here, but never this much.

He wondered how his dad could have had that much. Then, a thought formed in his head. He guessed it was all the money his dad got during the prohibition years. It had to be. Bernard was told many times that the generation before had nothing. His great-grandparents came on a boat from Spain with a sack of clothes and enough money to fit in the palm of a hand.

He remembered walking into Soto's Restaurant, which was the bar's name during that time. About seven years ago, the restaurant was dead. A few waiters stood around trying to act busy by wiping tables. That was when Bernard went to a door in the back that led down some stairs. He used the key his dad gave him to get into the door. His only need for going down there was to pay his dad a visit, but he never got that far.

The storage room was stuffed with people. Since Bernard had a key, the man at the front was surprised by his entrance without the specific knocks. Men in pin-striped suits and women in evening gowns, even though it was the middle of the afternoon. Everyone was purchasing alcohol from a small bar set up in the corner. Some people were sitting around small tables with cards in their hands and stacks of cash and coins ready to bet. He knew his dad was around there somewhere, but he was too hard to find. There were so many people in such a small space that it was getting hard to breathe. All Bernard could smell was booze, smoke, and sweat. He decided to talk with his dad later. In fact, he decided never to go down there again because he knew it was like that every day.

Bernard knew that was why the safe was so full. That also proved why his dad never spent it. They could have afforded a nicer house or more land; even a few more animals would have been nice to have on their farm. It seemed like Mr. Soto never spent too much money. Bernard remembered opening two gifts every Christmas and birthday, one big and one small. They went out to eat once a month, and shopping was only meant for necessities. But now he understood what an impact that time had on his family, and he was grateful things were starting to get back to normal.

Bernard turned the dial three times and then decided on the new safe code that only the two of them would know. He latched the lever on the back of the door and closed it shut. The new combination was set, signifying that everything belonged to George and him now. Thinking about George, Bernard walked to the opposite wall in the office and picked up the phone. He inserted his index finger into the first hole and moved it in a circle, repeating the motion until he had dialed the number to the grocery store and asked for George. Albert, one of the workers, answered, "Sorry, sir, he's not here."

"What do you mean he is not there? Where is he?"

"I'm not sure. He said he had something important to do and will be back soon."

"Well, how long ago was this?" Bernard asked as his voice got louder with each word.

"It's been about an hour."

"An hour?"

He lost his temper and hung up the phone on Albert, a cashier who had been working for their family for over fifteen years. It's good to know that later that week, Bernard went to the store to apologize to Albert for being so angry.

Bernard thought the worst of George, thinking he must not be taking his job seriously if he plans on leaving all the time. Bernard started to walk back and forth in his new office at a steady pace. "That little shit. This is just like him. He messes up, and I get blamed or have to pick up the pieces. Just like in school."

As soon as Bernard stopped pacing, he started for the grocery store. With no manager there, he needed to ensure everything was okay. The store was about a mile away, right on the corner of where Main Street ends. Bernard was walking at a fast speed. He made sure to wave hello to his barber at Bucky's Barbershop and Eleanor on her morning walk; although she usually wanted to stop and gossip about her neighbors, she could tell Bernard needed to get somewhere.

Bernard noticed that the jewelry store had a new sign on their front window. He would have read what it said, but at that moment, he saw George through the window; he was standing at a counter and looking at jewelry.

"This is what you are doing when you are supposed to be working?" Bernard asked as he stormed through the door like he had just run a marathon.

"Ah, *bienvenido, Señor* Soto," said Carlos from behind the counter.

"*Hola.*" Bernard quickly acknowledged Carlos and looked back at George.

"Come over here, Bernard. Look at what I am thinking about buying."

Curious, Bernard walked closer. He saw George holding a gold ring with a rhombus-shaped blue gemstone on the top.

"Blue is her favorite color."

"George, what the hell are you doing?"

"What does it look like? I'm getting a ring for Minnie. I'm gonna ask her to marry me."

Bernard, surprised and angry, couldn't come up with words for both of those feelings, so he gave his brother a handshake. George took it as a congratulations.

"I know it's a new thing 'round here, but that's what she wanted."

"Geez, she asked for a gold ring? You sure about this girl?"

George gave him a shove. "Well, what do you think of it? Do you think she will like it?"

"Yeah, you're making others look bad. I didn't do this for Susan. My God, George, how much is it?"

"I've got it taken care of. Besides, I got a good job now."

"Which you are not at, by the way. You need to be serious about working. I am not going to pick up your slack. You are the manager now, and you have to show your employees a good example by being a hard worker."

"*Calma, papá.*"

Bernard shrugged, loathing that George was mocking him. George knew that he should not have left work, but the shop would close early, and he could not wait another day to get this ring. Excitement was overwhelming him. The brothers walked back down the street together. George apologized for leaving work for so long.

"So, when are you gonna ask the question?"

"Tomorrow."

Before Bernard could say anymore, he remembered why he wanted to talk to George in the first place.

"I need to tell you something. That's why I called for you earlier."

George nodded, and Bernard double-checked they were alone on the street.

Bernard whispered in his brother's ear, "Twelve. Seven. Thirty."

George looked up as if he was writing those numbers in his brain. "Good choice."

CHAPTER THREE

George phoned Ruben and asked if he wanted to meet for a drink after work. He agreed and said that he would never turn down a drink. The two met at the bar right as Bernard had packed up his things and left his office. Ruben watched as he locked the office door behind him. Bernard noticed his watchful eyes, then walked out of the bar without another glance in his direction.

"How are you all doing with the new ownership?" Ruben questioned George.

"Well, Bernard got pissed today, but it was worth it."

"Really, Bernard? Angry?" Ruben asked sarcastically.

They both gave a small laugh. "He got angry at you?"

"I left work for a while."

Ruben smirked. "That's just about the number one rule in the Soto family. You go to work, you stay at work, and you go home. Then you do it all over again until you die."

"Yeah, well, I was picking up something." George pulled the ring out of his pocket. When he passed it to Ruben, the gem shined as it hit the light from the window.

"Man, is this what I think it is?"

"Yep, I am gonna ask her tomorrow. I just wanted to fill you in on it first."

"That's great, *hermano*. Look at you going fancy. People would think you're a big city chap. I am happy for you." Ruben inspected the ring and slid out of the booth with the ring sitting in his palm.

"Hey, where are you going?" George asked with his arm stretched out, trying to grab ahold of Ruben.

"Oh, just going to go pawn this."

George chuckled nervously. "Give it back."

"Just messing. I wouldn't do that. So how much was it?" Ruben asked, sliding back into his seat.

"Let's just say she is worth every penny."

Ruben placed the ring back in George's hand and said his goodbyes. George noticed his face as he walked out the door. It was a face he hadn't seen in a while. Desperation.

When George picked Minnie up the next day in his grandpa's 1920 Chrysler coupe, cherry red, with more power than the family truck that he usually drives, she knew it was a special occasion. George's dad only drove it for nice dinners with his wife or for family birthdays. She also knew because George asked her out to dinner and told her to dress up to the nines. She wore a silk purple dress that came down a little past her knees, small black heels, and a white fur shawl.

George jumped out of the Chrysler and opened the door for Minnie. He told her she looked beautiful while she slid into the car. With a roar of the engine, the car started and sped down the street. George had to speak up because of the noise the wind made through the windows.

"We're gonna make a quick stop before dinner at the apple orchards; I hope that's okay?"

"Sure thing," Minnie said.

The two drove further down Minnie's street in silence, listening to the sounds of the car. George made a left on Main Street and drove a few minutes out of town. The apple orchards stood about six miles outside of Bernalillo, but in this car, it would not take long. George's hands felt sweaty with anticipation. He felt relieved that the sun was starting to set.

By the time they reached the sign that said, "You are now leaving Sandoval County," the Chrysler rumbled. It was a sound that George had never heard before and one that scared Minnie. The car's speed dropped slowly, and it pulled itself to the left until George stopped it diagonally on the side of the street. George hopped out of the car and checked the tires. The left front tire was completely flat. George became angry and kicked the tire, forcing the entire car to sink further on its left side. The orchards were too far away, the town was too far away, and he had a ring in his pocket, a girl in a nice dress, and a car that looked like it had died. He slammed his hand down hard on the hood. He didn't have a spare attached to the car; in fact, the tire that was now deflated was the spare. He knew a spare is never reliable. He should have changed it a long time ago.

"Damn it," he screamed.

Minnie jumped out of the car. "Hey, it's okay. We can walk back to town and ask for a mechanic."

"The shops are all closed, and I really needed to get to the orchards."

"Why. Can't it wait till later?"

No. It couldn't wait. He planned out everything. The lighting was going to be perfect with the sun about to set, the ring was shiny, and the smell of apples would have hung around them as he asked her the question. It would have been what she wanted.

"No, it really couldn't wait."

"Well, why not? What aren't you telling me?"

They had been honest with each other so far, and George thought of no reason why he shouldn't tell her now.

"I was going to ask you a question."

Minnie smiled. She knew exactly what question it was going to be.

She turned away from the car, and for a few heartbeats, she watched the sun slide behind the mountains. George slouched over the hood of the car, trying to think of which way to start walking. His head was in the palm of his hand. He heard Minnie's footsteps and saw that she was standing in front of him.

"Ask me now."

"No, not like this." They were standing on the side of a dirt road, and with a slight stench of manure in the air, he could not imagine it going well. After she pleaded with him a few more times, George pulled the ring out of his pocket, sunk down on one knee, and grabbed Minnie's hand. "Minnie, my love, will you marry me?"

"Yes, I will definitely marry you, George Soto."

He rose and placed the blue-gemmed ring on her finger. They kissed in front of the tilted car that would take them nowhere. That didn't matter. They knew exactly what their future would hold. The two walked back to town, holding hands and talking about their next steps.

On his walk home, George could already imagine his parents' faces as he told them about that night's events. First, they both would be thrilled, his mom especially, as she would have tears running straight down her face, and his dad would give him a firm congratulatory handshake. Then, his mom's face would be worried once he told them about the car tire, and his dad would be furious.

It turns out that is exactly how it happened. George's dad said he should have checked the tires before even thinking about driving it, and his mom calmed him down by thanking the Lord that they both were not hurt. George was sent to his room like when he was a child. He was thankful that soon he would no longer have to live with his parents and could start a life of his own.

The next morning, his father's attitude completely altered. He said he was going to get the car fixed, and he already made a call to the mechanics to go pick it up off the side of the road. George couldn't believe it. It was usually Bernard cleaning up his mistakes, not his dad. He must have been in a good mood.

"I would also like to take you and Minnie out for a congratulatory dinner. Invite Bernard, Susan, and Beto, too."

"Are you sure, Dad? That sounds like a lot."

"Nonsense. I'm proud of you, *mijito*. This is the beginning of a new life. We will go to Whitey's."

Whitey's was one of the three restaurants in town, but it was definitely a swanky place. George knew his dad was in a good mood because he had only been there once in his life, and that was for his parents' fortieth anniversary.

The whole family got dressed in their nicest attire. Full dresses for the girls, and the boys, even little Beto, were sporting their nicest three-piece suits with a hat. It was the restaurant's policy that everyone looked their Sunday best. Minnie kept tugging on her dress. It was the same as the night before because it was the only upscale dress she owned.

"Stop it. You look beautiful," George told her.

Before she could reply, the owner of Whitey's rushed over to Mr. Soto.

"Lorenzo, it's good to see you. It's been too long." Both Bernard and George gave a confused look. It was strange hearing their father's first name. Everyone in town called him Mr. Soto. They guessed, with a greeting that informal, that he had known the owner for a long time.

"Good to see you, too, Gabe. We are here for a celebration. George is finally settling down."

"Well, congratulations. Come in. I will get you the best table in the house."

Gabe escorted the family to a large circle table in front of a stage where a band was playing some soft, light tunes. Everyone took their seats. Susan placed Beto in a booster seat next to her and Minnie.

"Soon, you will be having one of your own," Susan said to her.

"Oh, I hope so. They are such a blessing." She blushed.

George looked around. The restaurant wasn't too crowded. There were four other tables taken, mostly by husbands and wives and a few gentlemen drinking at the bar. He looked closer to find that one of those gentlemen was Ruben. As quick as a heartbeat, George excused himself and walked over. Ruben was sitting next to another man he had never seen before. They seemed to be in a deep conversation but stopped when Ruben noticed George getting closer.

"Georgie, what are you doing here?"

"Hey, we're celebrating with the whole family."

"Oh, here, at Whitey's? Your dad must be in a good mood. I've rarely seen him out."

George laughed and looked at the guy sitting next to Ruben. He was brunette, with light skin and light eyes. *This gringo is obviously not from around here*, George thought.

"Oh, sorry, how rude of me. George, this is a friend from California. I had to show him the nicest place in town."

"Brian," he said.

"It's nice to meet you. Are you just visiting?"

"Yeah, you could say that," he said with a deep but laid-back voice.

It became quiet, and George wondered if this was one of the bullies from California that Ruben barely mentioned the other night. He examined him some more, and George thought he wasn't. He looked nicer and even smaller than the bullies he dealt with on the playground.

"Well, listen, I'll let you two finish your drinks. It was nice meeting you." George walked away and sat back down with his family. His eyes kept wandering back to their conversation at the bar. He wondered why Ruben did not mention he would be going here tonight. The rest of the dinner was pleasant. They had steaks all around, except for Beto. He had a bowl of peas and carrots. He complained to his mom and dad several times about "no vegable." The "T" and "S" sounds were difficult for him then. George's parents told stories of their wedding and said how excited they are that both of their boys now have new lives. They gave Minnie and George their blessing, and Minnie said how grateful she was to be a part of a wonderful family. They ended the meal with slices of apple pie, made with apples from none other than Soto Orchards. As the family walked out, George said goodbye to Ruben.

"We'll see you later. Hey, where did your friend go?"

"Oh, he just left a minute ago. He has an early start in the morning," Ruben said, gesturing to the front door.

"Okay. Well, be safe. I'll see you later."

"See you," Ruben yelled.

Minnie, George, and his parents squished into the family truck. It was a Ford model, cheap, reliable, and it never had a flat tire. At least that's what George's dad said many times while driving to the restaurant. Minnie thanked his parents as they dropped her off at her place. When they pulled into their driveway minutes later, Mrs. Soto noticed the bedroom light was left on and shining through the window.

"I'm sorry, *mi amor*. I must have forgot," George's mom said as they opened the door to the house.

Mr. Soto was about to respond with an "it's okay," but she covered up his words with a big scream—such a hard sound on George's ears. The men rushed into the house and noticed what a mess it was. Cabinets were knocked over, drawers were pulled out, glass was everywhere, and the bedroom was the worst of all. The mattress was pulled up and thrown across the room. Mrs. Soto's jewelry box was empty, and clothes from the closet were scattered on the floor. They had been robbed. They went through every room. The fine china was still in the cupboards. The radio was on the shelf. It seemed to be just the jewelry.

"Did they take anything else besides Mom's jewelry?" George asked. His voice was shaky, and his face felt hot, as if it was injected with hatred.

Mr. Soto was frantic. He stood on a chair and looked through the top shelf of the closet.

"Yes, they got it."

"What?" George's mom blubbered through the tears.

"My gun. The Colt 45. The bastards took it."

CHAPTER FOUR

I t was on Mr. Soto's wedding day that his mother gave him the revolver. She handed it to him carefully before the wedding. He inspected the gun in his hands. It was silver, so shiny he could see part of his reflection. The handle was wooden, and when he flipped it over to the other side, it had the initials G.S. engraved into the wood.

"Are you sure, Mama?"

"Your dad wanted you to have it. His exact words would have been, 'You're starting your own family now, and you need to protect them. Family comes first.'"

"I wish he was here, especially today."

"Me too." His mom thought back to the day that her husband, the original George Soto, got a cold. Two weeks later, it turned into pneumonia. And as quick as a dream, he was gone.

Mr. Soto stood in his closet, looking stiff and angry, remembering how special that gun was to his father. He felt so connected to his father once he held that gun. As if his father would always be with him. Always there to protect him, even when he didn't need it.

The sheriff was called and started to search the house the next morning. George and his parents tried not to move anything as they didn't want to tamper with evidence. Mrs. Soto, furious that all her jewelry was taken, said it was lucky that she didn't have much in the first place. A long pearl necklace, a small gold pinky ring, and two pairs of earrings were taken. One was a pair of diamond stud earrings, and the other was small emeralds. The rest of her jewelry she had worn to dinner that evening.

The sheriff, a shorter gentleman with a full mustache that slightly curled at the ends, searched the entire house, not just the rooms that were rummaged through. He informed George and his parents that he wouldn't rest till he solved the case.

"Well, they had to have known we were all out to dinner, so doesn't that mean someone must have seen the whole family out together?" Mrs. Soto asked, putting the pieces together.

"It had to have been someone at the restaurant or someone that saw us driving there." Mr. Soto glared at George. It was a look that he tried to use on Bernard and him when they were kids to get them to fess up to something they did. Bernard would always protect George and take the fault. Like when George was nine and forgot to shut the farm gate, the sheep got loose and wandered down the street. The two boys ran down the road on a sheep hunt. After they were corralled and moved back home, George was too afraid of their dad's look, so Bernard said he was the one who forgot to shut it. That's just the kind of big brother he always was.

"Dad, I know what you are thinking, and just stop. Ruben and his friend were there the entire time. He said his friend left a minute or two before us. There is no way. Besides, I think his thieving days are over. He was just a kid. You need to let it go—" George noticed his defensiveness and stopped his rant.

"I didn't say anything. I'm just trying to figure this out, just like your mom."

George excused himself because he felt tension between him and his father. He heard his mom thanking the Lord in Spanish, saying she was glad no one was hurt. He left for his room, which was not harmed. He lay on his bed and tried to think of someone who would do something like that. What did they need a few pieces of jewelry for and the gun? How did they know there would be a gun? *Desperation*, he guessed. The need to sell the jewelry for money.

He tried to think of the last time he was in desperate need of something. It took him a while. Nothing seemed to appear. That's the thing; desperation, it happens so often to some, while others never experience it.

CHAPTER FIVE

"I think I know who did it," Bernard confessed to his family the next day after. They sat at the dining table, and he said he heard about the incident from Eleanor, who walks her dog by Bernard's house every morning. Naturally, the whole town knew of last night's events.

"It was Chuck. I fired him yesterday."

"Our bartender? Chuck has been working there forever," Mr. Soto said. Not in a loud voice yet, but it was getting there. He had always respected Chuck. Mr. Soto and Chuck were about thirteen years apart. He had a dark complexion and always wore a wool cap ever since he started to lose his hair. His dad hired him when he was a teenager, and he worked his way up to lead bar boy.

"Well. You don't know the whole story. Things have been getting hard there since I took over. Some regular customers stopped coming in, and the ones who do often just ignore me. Chuck doesn't listen to me and never greets me."

"So, you just up and fire someone for not listening to you or not saying hi to you? It has only been a few days, Son."

"It's not like that, Dad. He always respected you. When I walk in there, he stops working like he goes on strike or something. Someone will ask him for a drink, and he will tell the customer to go ask Daddy's boy. He makes jokes to the customers about what I had to do to get the job, and they just find it funny. One time, I asked to get a Coca-Cola from the bar, and he slid it so far and fast down the bar to where I was sitting that the bottle broke, and glass went everywhere. I asked him to clean it up, and he left it for me to clean after work."

George had no idea that his brother was having such a hard time adjusting. Things at the grocery store were smooth sailing for him. Customers enjoyed seeing him. One older lady even brought him homemade cookies. He felt bad. During his whole childhood, Bernard seemed to have everything together. He was the type to be organized in every aspect of his life. This was probably harder for him than he let on.

"So, about two days ago, I asked to speak to him in your office. I mean my office. So, he went in there with his pompous attitude, and I asked if he could respect me more around the customers. I asked if he would work harder while I am around. I said if he didn't, he would be fired. He gave a smirk and walked out. The next day, he pulled the same trick. It was early, so the band was still playing softer tones. I was trying to talk to the customers, you know, get to know them a bit more. When I asked Chuck for another round of drinks for them, he ignored it. So, I asked again. After plenty of time, he brought them over and spilled one on my pants. So, right there, I fired him. He threw a fit and stormed out, saying this joint will never be the same."

Bernard finished. You could tell he felt horrible about what he had done. Mr. Soto sat still on the sofa. He looked up at Bernard and said, "I am proud of you, Son. You stood your ground. You have worked hard to get where you are, and if someone is not respecting that, then they shouldn't waste your time."

"But look what he did. It's my fault," Bernard said, pointing to the cabinets that needed to be lifted off the ground. Even a few pieces of glass still lay around, catching the sunlight from the nearest window.

"It's not your fault. You did what every good boss would do. I will tell the sheriff this, and we will leave the questioning to him. In the meantime, will you two boys help clean this place up?"

Bernard and George jumped up right away. Bernard could see the hurt in his dad's eyes, but confidence in who did this made them both feel slightly better. At this point, what he wanted more than anything wasn't to have Chuck arrested or to get justice. He wanted his dad's gun back.

Mr. Soto said he would leave it to the sheriff, but the revolver meant too much to him not to go over to Chuck's house that next morning. He pounded his fist on the front door repetitively until Chuck answered.

"Mr. Soto. Hey, how's it going?"

"Cut the crap. Where's my gun?"

"What are you talking about?" Chuck realized what he meant because Eleanor told him about the break-in too. "You don't think it was me, do you?"

"Let's just say you're on our list. Now give me my gun."

"Mr. Soto, please, you must believe me. I don't have your gun."

Mr. Soto believed him, but only after he pushed through the door and searched his house for the next thirty minutes. Chuck told him he wouldn't find anything, and Mr. Soto knew he didn't do it. Chuck was too relaxed; he even helped pull out drawers and open the closets to make his search easier.

"Sorry to mess up your things, Chuck."

"It's okay," Chuck said as he walked Mr. Soto out. "No hard feelings, right buddy?" Chuck stuck his hand out for a handshake.

Now, Mr. Soto was seventy-five years old, but when he punched Chuck in the nose, he felt like a young man again. As Chuck started bleeding, Mr. Soto said, "That's for my son."

Around the same time, Ruben slapped George on the back at the grocery store.

"Gosh, what was that for?"

"I can truly congratulate you now, *hermano*. You're not a free man anymore."

"Oh, thanks."

"What's the matter? Not excited to settle down?"

"No, I am. It's just that I'm still worried about everything that happened the other night."

"Oh, yeah." Ruben nodded. "Eleanor told me about the robbery."

George rolled his eyes. *That lady should write a gossip column for the newspaper*, he thought. *She is the only news source in this town.*

"I'm sorry, though. Do you all know who did it?"

"No, we're still trying to figure it out."

"Well, I'll keep my eyes and ears open. Hey, I also heard Chuck was fired."

"Yeah, we are going to start interviewing soon for his replacement."

"Hey, well, what about me?"

George tried as hard as he could, but he couldn't hold his laughter in. He knew Bernard would never let that happen. He also had a funny feeling that history would repeat itself with Ruben behind the bar, so he thought up something else to say.

"Oh, well, it's just that we wanted to hire one of the cleanup boys just cause, you know, they've paid their dues."

Ruben nodded and squinted. George hoped that he believed that, but there was no telling.

A few boxes fell from one of the shelves, and George ran to pick them up. He looked stressed. The store was busy, there was a robber on the loose, and now boxes were randomly falling.

"Hey, George, I think you need a night away from this. Let's go have a bonfire like we used to. Besides, I want to congratulate you and Maddy together."

"Her name is Minnie, but okay, that might be nice."

"Great, I'll ask Lesley to pick her up tonight, and we will all meet there."

"Yeah, sure, that's fine." He got even more stressed when he saw the line at the front of the store. "Hey, I better help out. It's getting pretty crowded over there." George pointed to the front of the store.

"Okay, I'll pick you up at eight then?"

George nodded and opened a new line for impatient customers.

CHAPTER SIX

With pen and paper, Mr. Soto started a list. A list of everyone he could think of that he might have pissed off. He was not happy with how long the list was, but *it is what it is*, he thought. Maybe that time he punched some thief at the orchards for stealing a few apples was a bit too far. Or maybe it goes back to the time he cussed out some kids for waiting outside the bar door and tripping older drunk men with string. Maybe those kids were all grown and wanted payback. He knew his anger was never his best quality.

Mrs. Soto walked in crying again. Her eyes seemed permanently flooded and red for days.

"Is everything okay? Did they take something else?"

"No." She calmed down at bit. "No, I'm just happy they didn't take this masterpiece."

She was holding a piece of parchment. It was a family portrait that George drew when he was seven years old. There was Mr. and Mrs. Soto, looking closer to potatoes than actual humans, but they were holding hands. Then, a slightly shorter potato was Bernard. He was playing with what she guessed was one of their sheep. Finally, there was a very small potato with fuzzy hair, which must have been the artist himself. She let out a giggle. The frame Mrs. Soto placed it in was broken, but the drawing inside was as new, and that is all that mattered.

Mr. Soto saw the small smile she gave him, and he began to worry about the stress this caused her heart. For many years now, she complained of heart palpitations but refused to see a doctor. Every time she clutched her chest, Mr. Soto seemed to have a mild heart attack himself.

He thought back to a month ago, which was the last time this happened.

"Please see a doctor," he pleaded with her.

"Why would I do that? Pay all that money just for some old *gringo* to tell me I am just getting older."

"No, that old *gringo* could probably help. Maybe at least give you something to calm down the worrying."

Mrs. Soto raised her hands. "What am I worried about? I have everything I need. Two wonderful boys, a stubborn husband, and this beautifully clean house with everything I need in it."

Now that he was looking back on that conversation, the irony of that last part stung. At that moment, though, he recalled the stubborn husband part.

"I'm not that stubborn."

Mrs. Soto could not hold back the laughter, so much that a few more tears came to her eyes. She wiped them away and said, "The sad part is, I think you actually believe that, *mi amor*."

"I just like things in my way."

"But eventually, you need to let things go and pass them on to those more capable."

"We're obviously talking about the businesses."

"Obviously." She huffed.

"I will let the boys run them. Just give me a few more years."

"You said the same thing a few years ago."

He thought back. "I did, didn't I?" He thought again on the matter. "I guess we're not getting any younger. And they do seem ready. At least Bernard is."

"You know George is ready too."

"He has been stepping up. Oh, and this way, I can be home and take care of you."

"Lorenzo Juan Soto."

Oh, she used the full name, he thought. *What did I say that deserved the full name?* That was only used when she was upset. He gave her a confused look.

"I want you to retire for you. I do not need taking care of. I have cooked, cleaned, raised two boys, and kept this house afloat for years; I am mighty fine continuing to do that. I do not need doctors or you to tell me anything."

"Then why do you need me home?"

She waved her hands at him and started to walk out of their living room.

Now, looking back on this conversation and noticing the mess their house was in, he finally put the pieces together. He always told her that it took him a while to understand what he said wrong. Though, this time was extremely long. While she was looking for a new frame for George's work of art, he grabbed her hands and said, "Mary, I'm happy I stepped down from everything. Now we have the rest of our lives to just be together."

CHAPTER SEVEN

It was no surprise that George wasn't completely listening to Ruben's final words at the grocery store. So, when Ruben honked outside the Soto house, George hurried to the bathroom, changed into pants, slipped on suspenders and shoes, and rushed out the door. He was in such a hurry that he forgot to tell his parents where he was going and who he was going with. They won't care, he thought. He could see they were having some sort of moment—holding hands and just looking at each other.

When he got to the car, he noticed that Brian, the guy he met at Whitey's the other night, was in the front seat. George thought he would be riding shotgun, but instead, he slid into the back seat. He noticed the stench of whiskey from both of them. Looking over the front seat, one large half-empty whiskey bottle confirmed the smell. Brian sported the same suit he was wearing at the restaurant. It got quiet when he pulled himself in and shut the door, almost like he interrupted another important conversation. Ruben started his dad's Buick, pulled out on the road, and headed for empty land. That was the usual spot for bonfires they had back when they were in school.

George broke the silence. "It's nice to see you again, Brian."

"Yeah, same here, little Mexican."

There was another burst of silence. *That was strange*, George thought. Ruben had a much lighter complexion than George, but they came from the same background. He figured the Californian must have been somewhat prejudiced.

"Want a swig, Georgie?" Ruben asked while lifting the bottle by its neck.

"No, thanks. I'll wait till we get there. So, Ruben, you are sure your cousin is gonna pick up Minnie? I haven't been able to call her all day because the store was so busy."

Ruben nodded while driving. "Oh, sure thing. She'll be there."

The rest of the ride went by in silence. It was odd for Ruben to be so quiet. He was always the chatty one in their group of friends. George remembered getting in trouble in school for always talking to Ruben in the back of the class. Ruben usually took the blame, but George insisted they sit in detention together since they were both talking and both should be punished.

The drive was long, but at least no flat tires this time. They passed the orchards and kept driving about ten more minutes before Ruben decided to stop and pull into the empty land. It was mostly dirt and bushes, but it had tons of room to build a fire, drink, and talk with friends. They each got out of the car and started looking for a good spot.

"Hey, shouldn't you have left your lights on so the girls can find us?" George asked Ruben, anticipating his fiancé's arrival.

"Ah, no, they know where we're at," he said before taking another giant gulp of whiskey. By this time, there was only a few ounces left in the glass bottle. Ruben had been hogging it the entire drive, and George was wondering why Brian never asked for another sip.

"Okay, what about the wood? You did bring firewood, right?"

Neither Ruben nor Brian said anything. They walked a little further into the desert. Ruben was stumbling through the dirt as if he just got off a boat that had been out at sea. The moon and stars were enough lighting; they could still see each other surrounded by a few plants and cacti.

"Just do it," Brian said.

Ruben gave him a worried look.

Three unexpected things happened that night. One, Minnie never came. Two, George was left out in the desert. Three, Ruben betrayed him.

"Ruben, do this, or you will regret it," Brian yelled at him.

"Why don't we just have a conversation first?" Ruben pleaded.

"What the hell is wrong with you? Just get it over with."

At that moment, Ruben took a gun out of his pocket and pointed it at George. It wasn't just any gun. Though he had only seen it a few times, he knew it was his grandfather's revolver, with the same initials on the side that were used for his name too.

"What are you doing with that?" George said in complete shock.

Ruben didn't answer.

"Come on. Stop kidding around. What's going on?"

"We need something from you, George, and we're not leaving here until I get it," Brian demanded.

George looked at Ruben and saw the madness in his friend's eyes. He noticed the desperation in his voice, but he couldn't put it all together as to what drove him to this point.

"What's the number to the safe in the office?"

George looked hurt and flustered. He said, "What are you talking about? How did you get the gun?"

Ruben took his index finger and wrapped it around the trigger. "What's the number to the safe in the office? I'm not going to ask again."

Why did he need the money in the safe? How did he know there was a safe? How did he know that they had changed the code? So many questions went through George's mind. George saw that Brian was coaching Ruben through this. He said he had to do this, that it had to be done. When Ruben slowly lowered the gun, Brian forced him to bring it back up with just a few words.

"The boss isn't gonna like it if he doesn't get his money, and the jewelry ain't gonna cover it," said Brian.

George thought of a solution and told them a code. "Okay, okay. You win. It's a combination of Bernard and Beto's birthdays."

That was a lie, but he knew they wouldn't believe him if there wasn't some significance behind the code. So, he gave them a code using Bernard's birthday month, eight, and Beto's birthday month and day, eleven and twenty-five.

"Why would you do this?" George yelled.

"There are some things you don't understand," Ruben said as Brian ran to the car to get some rope out of the trunk.

"You could have just asked me for money. A loan or something."

Ruben chuckled. "Yeah, just like I asked for a job. Besides, like you have money. Your dad has the cash, and he wouldn't give me a dime. He can't even look at me."

George knew they would be back once they found out the numbers were wrong; that's why the *gringo*, Brian, thought of the rope. George struggled as much as he could. He tried to punch Ruben in the gut, but the two men held every limb and tied him up. They had enough rope to cover most of his body. They started for the car, leaving George constricted but alive.

Fear and panic consumed George's every thought. The entire time they were gone, he squirmed around like a worm trying to escape the ropes. There was no use. He yelled, but he knew that would be no use either. He then thought of snakes, coyotes, and even werewolves. *I'm going to be eaten alive*, he figured. He used all his strength, even his teeth ripping through rope threads. Headlights started to peak over the hill. He found some hope. He was almost out of the ropes. *That could not be them*, he thought. They could not have driven to town, broken in, tried the code, and driven back in that short of time. Now completely free from the ropes, he thought he was safe. He pictured his dad or brother coming to look for him.

It wasn't his family. It was them.

CHAPTER EIGHT

George was free and started running back into the desert, looking for anywhere to hide. He tripped a few times on a cactus and then some brush. The sky's stars were so bright that anywhere he hid, they would find him. Brian tackled him to the ground. He gave him two punches to the face. With each punch, George saw the night sky get even darker. George wrestled him to his back and gave him one punch back. Brian kneed him in the groin, stood up, and kicked him in the gut.

"Enough," Ruben yelled, still holding his family's gun in one hand and the now empty whiskey bottle in the other.

"Ruben, just stop! This is bullshit."

"Sorry, *hombre*. There are some things I need to do."

"Well, what is it? I can help you."

"Not this time. I got into too much trouble this time. Ten grand worth."

George panicked. Even if he did give them the correct code, he didn't think they had that much in the safe. He was still kneeling in the dirt and looked up at his old friend. Ruben had tears in his eyes, and his hand was shaking around the gun.

"Georgie, you know I love you, but I have to do this. Give me the real code, and no one will get hurt."

"You know I can't do that. That money stays in the family."

"I thought we were family."

"If we were family, you wouldn't be holding that gun right now."

Brian walked around and whispered in Ruben's ear, coaching him again. He stepped back and gave Ruben a nudge.

Ruben blubbered through the tears, "If you don't give me the real numbers, I'll be forced to shoot you."

"If you shoot me, how will you get the money you need?"

Brian whispered into Ruben's ear, "Give it a few days, and there'll be reward money for anyone who knows anything. We'll collect then."

"I won't give it to you. You don't want to do this," George yelled.

Brian said, "Just do it. It's not a crime to kill one of them."

"One." Ruben started counting. Assuming he was going to end with three, George was shaking all over, afraid of what would happen; he would choose to die rather than give up his family's hard-earned money.

"Two"

"Ruben, come on. You know family comes first."

"I thought we were family, brother."

George put his head down and gave up, realizing the new life he had planned for just a few days prior would never happen.

"Do it. He already knows too much," Brian yelled.

"Three." With a twitching hand, Ruben pulled the trigger, striking George's skull. George's body fell back and hit the ground hard enough to create a cloud of dirt.

Ruben placed the gun in George's right hand and the empty bottle of whiskey in the other to make it look as if they were never there.

They drove back to town, leaving George's distinctly positioned body frozen in the moonlight.

CHAPTER NINE

"When was the last time you saw George?" Mr. Soto asked one of his former employee's at the grocery store.

"Uh, about two days ago, I believe."

After not hearing from George for a full day, Minnie, George's parents, Bernard, and the same curly-mustached sheriff searched the entire town. They tried to put the pieces together again. The bar was broken into, and although nothing was taken, it was no coincidence that George went missing on the same night. When Bernard went in the next morning, the bar's doors were broken, and the office was torn apart. Bernard checked the safe just to be sure, and everything else in the bar remained there. George's mom looked ill from worry while the rest of the family tried to calm her down. She did find it strange that George didn't say goodbye or tell them whom he was going with.

They asked people at the bar, they checked at popular businesses down Main Street, and they even asked Eleanor and found all the same answers. They all barely remember the last time they saw him.

"That leaves one last person we need to ask," Mr. Soto told his family, "but I would like to go alone."

They all understood. When he got to Ruben's family home, his sister answered the door. She was about fourteen years younger than Ruben and still in grade school. She loudly called for Ruben after Mr. Soto asked to speak to him. Ruben looked ten years older. He had big, black bags under his red eyes. He wore wrinkled slacks and walked barefoot to the door. His eyes widened as he saw Mr. Soto standing at the front door.

"Mr. Soto, this is a surprise," he said somewhat naturally.

"It is?"

"Well, yes, I don't see you out much anymore."

"You don't look well," Mr. Soto said, analyzing each word Ruben murmured.

"Oh, it's just a cold, I think. How can I help you?"

"I am looking for my son. Have you seen him?" Mr. Soto didn't take his eyes off Ruben's. He knew that Ruben's answer was false because he didn't look him straight in the eye as he told him, "No, no, I haven't, sir."

"When was the last time you saw him?"

Again, his eyes twitched to the side, then back down to the ground.

"I picked him up a few nights ago for a drive, but then I brought him home about an hour later."

"I see. Well, let us know if you hear from him."

"Sure thing, sir. Thanks for stopping by." Ruben shut the door a little too quickly.

On his walk home, Mr. Soto knew he was lying. He was always good at that. His sons could never lie to him. He constantly knew when Bernard was taking the blame for George or when George lied about staying late to play at school when he was really in detention with the same liar that he had just spoken with.

Days went by, and the family became more worried. They were desperate, and they needed to come up with something instantly. The investigation wasn't going anywhere. Mrs. Soto was constantly pacing, never resting.

They decided there needed to be a reward. The family made posters and posted them all around town. With a stack of posters, hammers, and nails, Mr. and Mrs. Soto, Bernard, and even Minnie made their way around the town. Each poster said a 1,000-dollar reward for anyone who knows the whereabouts of George Soto.

The very next day, news started to arrive. Calls came in, and people came to their door saying they saw him, but no one had proof. People were desperate for the money; little did they know that the reward was most of the family's money that they had on them.

About a week later, something promising came to their door.

"Honey, the sheriff is here," Mrs. Soto said as he walked through the front door. He noticed all the candles that his wife lit. She believed they would help George find his way home. He imagined her lighting every single one each day and saying a short prayer afterward.

"Hello, Mr. Soto." They shook hands. "I have some news for you two, but you may want to sit down."

They obeyed.

"First off, we found your son."

The Sotos looked relieved. Mrs. Soto was ready to blow out all her candles, but they did not let the officer finish.

"Please," he said, "let me finish." He stroked the curled end of his mustache with a hint of nervousness in his voice. "A man came into the station saying he wanted the reward as he had real proof of your son's whereabouts."

Mrs. Soto asked, "Well, who was it?"

"Some fella named Brian. That's all I could get out of him. I think he was spotted in town the last few weeks with Ruben Valdez."

At that moment, Mr. Soto knew something was wrong. He knew they should not have been happy a few seconds ago. Above all, he knew his son was not okay.

The sheriff said, "The man who found him said he was out hunting and found your son laying in the desert with a gun to his head and a bottle in his other hand."

"He wouldn't do that. He just got engaged. He was the happiest I have seen him in a while."

"My wife is right," yelled Mr. Soto, "and he doesn't own a gun!"

"It matches your description of the one stolen in the robbery."

Mrs. Soto was beside herself, drowning in tears, while Mr. Soto was doing his best to hold his back. "You can't honestly think George faked the robbery and stole the gun."

"Of course not. That is why we believe whoever stole the gun is responsible. We are doing our best down at the station to figure this out. I will let you know when we find something," the sheriff said and started to head out.

Mr. Soto walked him out.

"*Señor*, I'd like to name a suspect that I have in mind. Do you have the right to call him in for questioning?"

"Absolutely. Who is it?"

"Ruben Valdez. The real man that wanted the reward."

Mrs. Soto sat on the sofa when he walked back in. She looked pale and in complete agony. She couldn't bear the thought of having to tell Bernard and Minnie. So, she sat completely still, looking at the wall. Mr. Soto said he would go tell them, but it was only to get away from his wife so he could grieve alone. When he got in his car, he let it all out, banging on the wheel and screaming.

"He was my boy. My baby boy," he blubbered.

He went to Minnie's house first to break the news. When she answered the door, she was already crying. The secretary at the police station overheard what happened and paid her a visit to deliver the news. Mr. Soto was grateful for that because he didn't know how he could have told her that her soon-to-be husband would not be around anymore. He didn't stay long; it was too hard to see the poor girl so upset.

When he got to Bernard's, he knew he hadn't heard the news, so he asked to speak with him in his car. He didn't want to face Susan and

Beto just yet. For an hour, they sat in the car, trying to talk through the pain and not show any emotion. They were both told throughout their lives to be strong in sad times.

Bernard said, "Where's the gun now?"

"Still with the detective, along with his body. They need it all for evidence."

"We need to find who did it." His pain turned to rage. It was complete hatred, an emotion that could change a man.

"We will. I promise."

Bernard yelled, "I'm going to kill whoever did this."

His father looked at him with surprise. He had never heard his son speak with such disgust. Revenge seemed to be sweating out of him. Although he was worried for him, he understood his pain; he was feeling it too. "Well, *mijo*, I think I can help with that."

CHAPTER TEN

Ruben Valdez was asked to come into the station the next day for questioning done by Officer Olden, the father of the sons who used to pick on him and George. He was an older guy, but still frightening as hell. He would squint his eyes in a way that would make you think he was reading your mind and a scar on his right cheek that proved he was more than tough. Maybe that's why they kept him around, just to frighten people being questioned about a case.

Ruben looked worse than when Mr. Soto saw him. He looked as if he aged a few more years. His hair was a mess, he wore no cap or coat, and just walked in with a shirt, pants, and shoes as if he was in a hurry. He acted professional to Officer Olden and asked what was going on, as if he had no idea.

With his fingers tapping the arm of the chair and sweat running across Ruben's forehead, it did not take long for Olden to discover Ruben had something to do with the death of George. In fact, it only took a few questions for Ruben's story to completely fall apart.

They sat at a desk with one lightbulb directed slightly toward

Ruben. The rest of the room was dark as night. Ruben could barely see the officer behind the light. Officer Olden stared straight into Ruben's eyes, looking for more triggers of weakness. His arms crossed, his squint ready.

"I wanted to thank your friend for finding George, but unfortunately, we have no idea of his whereabouts."

"Oh, I think he went back home. He told me, though. I still can't believe it."

Officer Olden squinted. "Is that so?"

"Yes, sir."

"I hope it's okay, but I have a few questions for you. You said to Mr. Soto that you were with George a few nights back, and you went for a drive? Is that correct?"

"Yes, yes sir, that's correct."

"What day was that again?"

"Friday."

Officer Olden looked down at his notes. "We have on record that it was last Saturday."

Ruben nodded and agreed to that night as if trying to recall what night it happened.

"How long were you out for?"

"Oh, about an hour or so. I dropped him back off at his house."

"Well, after speaking with Mr. Soto, he said he stayed up late last Saturday, and George never came home. How could that be? Did you see him walk through his door?"

"Yes, of course I did. He walked right in the front door."

Officer Olden scanned his notes again, especially highlighting the part where Mr. Soto said every family member always used the back door to get into the house.

Ruben was flipping his story on the spot, but he wasn't confessing. Officer Olden tried another technique. It was something he hadn't used in a while, which was to lie to get them to tell the truth.

"And what about you? You went straight home afterward?"

"Yes."

"Because I spoke to your sister before you came in, and she remembers you being gone."

"Oh, she must not have checked my room. I was there all night."

"Really? Because Eleanor also said she saw you driving late that night down Main Street." That was the lie that made him confess.

Ruben wasn't angry with his sister or Eleanor. They had no idea what was going on. *They were just being good citizens*, he thought. His hands were completely wet, and his face was cherry red. It was no use. He could have blamed it on Brian, but then he would have been an accomplice, and he would have known about it before confessing. It was time to give up. In fact, after he confessed to shooting George, he felt somewhat relieved.

Officer Olden started yelling, "Why would you do that? Your own friend?"

"I got into a shitload of trouble. A lot of trouble."

Ruben then looked up, remembering his first experience with gangsters. Upon his move to Los Angeles, and in the smallest apartment you could imagine, he was ready to start a new life. Ruben's neighbor asked if he would like to go out to dinner one night. He was a little younger than him and much more ambitious. Little did he know that there would be no dinner but plenty of drinks. They reached a popular restaurant. Ruben's neighbor said slowly to the host, "Can we dine with a friend at a table in the back?" Apparently, saying that exact phrase got you into the gambling room, which was through a door down some dark stairs under the actual restaurant.

The room was packed with rows of round tables where men played blackjack and poker. Exotic dancers danced on a stage next to a live band. Ruben's neighbor said they were there to work. Although Ruben didn't want to hand drinks to men, he eventually enjoyed his time. He and his neighbor met the man in charge of service and proceeded to get dressed in black suits with white aprons. They both poured drinks and passed them around to the large men at the poker tables. Ruben's neighbor said that he had to pull a lot of strings to get this gig and he would thank him one day. Each man had a cigar in their mouth, a hand wrapped around a glass, and a gun sitting on the table next to him, which was loaded and ready for anything. Ruben took in every moment. He watched the men; they were tough, but they laughed, drank, smoked cigars, and gambled. Above all, he could tell that each one was powerful. Ruben, hungry for power and wealth above everything else in the world, knew, at that moment, that someday he was going to be one of those men.

"Unfortunately, when I finally got my seat at the table, I gambled everything I owned and some that I didn't. My first shot at it, and I acted like a child. I sat at one of the round tables with a fancy suit and confidence like I never had before. The men I played with ate everything I owned in a matter of minutes, and I walked away with nothing but shame."

Officer Olden shook his head.

"And they never forget," Ruben continued. "Those men will hunt you down. If you don't pay, then they'll kill you and hide the body just to prove their power to the next sucker that comes in. Then they burst into my apartment one night, beat me up, and threatened that I had one month to pay *him* back."

"So you couldn't think of anything else to do? You could have left town."

"I wanted to stay there. I knew I would make it one day. I just needed some money to pay them back. You have to understand that they were going to kill me. The threats kept coming; another member of his mob jumped me and punched me countless times in a back alley. They're ruthless and cynical. The day before I left, one of them knocked on my door. I was already on edge, so I opened it slowly to find a package on the footstep. Inside was a dead bird with a note that said, 'You're next.'"

"They should've just done it," Officer Olden spat.

"So, I needed a way out. A friend from back west came up with an idea to borrow some money."

"You had no intentions of borrowing anything."

"I did. I swear. That was the only way I agreed to the burglary."

"So, you broke into their house?"

At this point, Ruben was in tears. His face looked boiling hot. "No, the other guy, Brian, he did. He works for those men. He only found a few things of value but not the amount of money we needed. So, that's when we knew there had to be some sort of savings box or safe in the bar's office, just like everyone in town always suspected."

He took a break from speaking because he was getting hard to understand. Olden didn't offer a hanky or sympathy. He asked him to speak again.

"So, we just took a guess, and George confirmed there was a safe when he gave us fake numbers. We broke in, looked everywhere in the office for a safe, found it, then tried it. After I found out it was wrong, I lost my mind. You see, I got involved with the mob. I gambled away ten grand, except I never had that kind of money to gamble. I owed money to the wrong type of people. The boss gave me only one month to get his money back; if not, he was coming after me."

"So, you killed your best friend?"

"The pressure took over. This guy, Brian, was getting in my head as well as the whiskey. Brian said the boss would come after my family too. I wasn't thinking straight, and on the drive back to George, I got so angry. I couldn't think of another way out. I had to prove to Brian I was serious. George would never give up the real code, and as soon as he got back to town, he would have turned me in."

Olden was finished. He asked Ruben to place his hands out in front of him. He obliged. Ruben knew he had to pay for what he did. He figured jail would be the safest place for him. So, he followed Officer Olden to the cell they had in the back of the station. It was a holding place until he would be transferred to the state prison up north. As Olden looked in the cell, Ruben sat down and prayed for forgiveness. He was speaking not only to God but also to George.

CHAPTER ELEVEN

I t had been five days since Ruben's confession. The entire family was informed about the murderer. After receiving George's body, the family arranged a funeral. It was as if the entire town showed with many flowers and condolences. Mrs. Soto's health was failing even more. Everything was happening so fast. Every time Mr. Soto closed his eyes, it was as if life was zooming by in a blur. Officer Olden called him to the station on the sixth day after the confession. He didn't want to leave his wife. She had been on bed rest since the funeral, but he considered it and found that whatever Olden needed was important.

Mr. Soto told his wife he would be back shortly, and she said she would be fine even though she didn't look fine. She looked pale, cold, and above all, heartbroken.

When he reached the station, he walked straight into Olden's office, not even glancing toward the back where Ruben sat in his cell. He sat down in the chair across from his desk.

"Thank you for coming. Now that the case is closed, I have no reason to keep this."

Officer Olden slid Mr. Soto's gun across the table with the initials G.S. pointing right at him as if they were asking him to take it. The gun that once meant so much to him was now tainted with bad memories. It made Mr. Soto want to throw it in the trash and have nothing to do with it. The initials now meant something else to him.

"Just keep it. I don't want it. I can't even look at it." It was as if the gun was stained with George's blood. Mr. Soto looked toward the wall. His dad meant so much to him, and that gun was proof that his dad's memory would always be with him, protecting him. But it wasn't protection anymore. It was death and hatred.

It was through this thought process that he remembered Bernard wanting revenge. He recalled the desperation in his son's eyes and the desire to hunt down the person who did this. It was mad, but who was he to judge how people grieved? Bernard was in pain, and this gun could help him. What was he thinking? Giving his son a loaded weapon, the same one that killed his own brother.

"This gun meant so much to you and your family. You should have it. Remember, it was not the gun that killed your son."

Olden's words made sense to Mr. Soto. He grabbed the gun and placed it in his coat's inside pocket. He thanked Olden for what he did on this case. While walking out of the office, he looked over at the cell in the back of the station. He asked Olden, who was right behind him, "When is he going up to the state prison?"

"Tomorrow night, sir."

"Good to hear." Mr. Soto charged toward the cell. He hadn't ran in a while, but he looked as if he was ready to kill. He banged on the bars of the cell and looked Ruben straight in his eyes. Confessing to the crime may have done him some good because he looked like he had finally got some sleep. Mr. Soto gripped one of the bars with his hand. Wrapping his fingers around the cold bar and squeezing hard, he pretended it was Ruben's throat. Ruben stood from his perched position on the ground. His lips started to move, and they looked like they were forming the words *I'm sorry*. Mr. Soto did not give him the satisfaction of noticing the apology; instead, he spat in his face. "*Cobarde*," he told him, and he was right. He was a coward. Mr. Soto was too hurt and disgusted to look at him any longer, so he unclenched his hand, slammed on the bars one more time, and left the silent station in a rage, where everyone inside was ready for what they thought was going to be another murder.

Mr. Soto's next stop was Bernard's place. They decided to talk in the car and not let Beto see what his grandfather was giving his dad.

"Bernard," his dad said softly and with concern, "I'm only giving you this because, well, one, I can't bear to look at it, and I was going to hand it down to you soon, anyway, and two, you sounded like you needed it for your own healing. But, Son, I must ask you not to do anything drastic. Please don't let your hatred right now ruin the rest of your life."

"Dad, you don't understand. I need to do this. He is my younger . . . or he *was* my younger brother."

"But Son, I don't want you to mess up things for your family. Besides, he is being taken up state tomorrow night."

Bernard looked up as if he was taking notes in his head. He was trying to think of a plan.

"Dad, I was always the one there for George. Whenever he got in trouble at school or at home, I tried to cover it up. I tried to take the blame. I did that because I never wanted to see him hurt or in pain or sad. I loved him that much. So, this"—he grasped the gun—"this will help. I need to protect George. I know it won't make sense to you, but I need to protect him, even though he is already gone."

Mr. Soto took a long deep breath. "I'm not stopping you, Son. If you feel this is what you need to do, I am just asking you to be careful. Remember, family comes first."

When Bernard held the gun in his hands, he felt safe—he had something to shield him from danger. Any other weapon in the world would not give him this type of feeling. The look on his face made his father even more concerned.

"Bernard, why does it have to be this?" he asked while looking down at the weapon.

He said the same thing that Officer Olden said. "It wasn't this that killed my brother. Besides, this gun has kept you safe. It will keep me safe too."

When Mr. Soto got home, he ran to his wife's bedside. He wasn't about to tell her what he had done the past hour. So, he asked how she was feeling.

"I'm fine. Just needed some rest," she muttered, still looking pale and cold but surprisingly a little less sad. "Now, move out of the way. I have to fix some supper."

"You don't have to do that."

"What?" She turned. "Are you going to take up cooking around here?"

"I just meant . . . are you sure you are up for that?"

"Of course, *mi amor*. Besides, George will be hungry when he gets home."

Mr. Soto froze. He thought he heard her wrong. "Honey, did you say you would make food for George?"

"Well, yes, he is always so hungry when he comes home from work."

"Oh, *mi amor*." He sat his wife down at the kitchen table, pulled up a chair next to her, and placed his hands over hers. "George isn't here with us anymore."

"Well, where did he go?"

"He passed away a little over a week ago."

As if her face hit a wall, it all came back to her. What happened now that she finally slept? She thought it all must have been a nightmare. She came back to the realization that she was not in her right mind and that her son was dead. She fell onto the kitchen floor and cried for the remainder of the night while her husband held and rocked her until she slept.

CHAPTER TWELVE

Bernard waited outside the station for the police car that would transport Ruben to the state prison. He had been waiting since late in the afternoon, but now that it was getting dark, he knew it should be any time now. He had a plan—or somewhat of a plan. Plan A—shoot Ruben as the officer puts him into the police car. That one was risky because he could miss and shoot the officer instead. Plan B—ask the officer for help with his car on the other side of the street and, while he is not looking, go and shoot Ruben. Plan C—go into the station and shoot Ruben in his cell in front of everyone. That one was not a good plan and probably not the one he would go with.

He knew his plans were fatal, both for Ruben and himself. They each involved being seen by an officer, but he was desperate from the pain of losing his brother who was more like a best friend. The only thing on his mind was killing the person who did this no matter the consequences.

Bernard would never hurt a fly. He was the nice guy in school and the one always picked last in school sports. Not because he wasn't good—he was all right—but because he was just not aggressive enough to play on a team. Bernard never minded losing as long as he had a good time. But now, with a family and business of his own, he would never think about murdering anybody—until now.

A police car pulled up and parked outside. The officer got out. He'd have to decide his plan soon. He decided to wait until he saw Ruben come out in handcuffs with the officer he assumed would drive him. He looked at his watch and noticed that fifteen minutes had gone by. It could not possibly take that long to get a prisoner out of a cell and put him into a car. He decided to wait another fifteen minutes. It was fully dark by the time he became impatient and stormed into the station holding the gun.

Officers sitting at their desks looked at him like he was crazy, but to their benefit, he did look a little insane. His eyes were red with anger and his hand clinched, ready around the gun by his side. The officer closest pulled out his gun. "Put it down, Son," he yelled. Bernard started walking slowly to the back and looked through the cell when he realized no one was in there. He became worried that he would be put in there next if he didn't calm down, so he placed the gun in his suit jacket pocket and politely asked for Officer Olden. A few officers pointed to his office and carefully watched Bernard walk across the room. Bernard knocked on the door and walked in.

"You're here late. Didn't think you worked this late?" Bernard asked Olden.

"Only when I think people are gonna come in with a gun ready to kill someone. What are you doing, Bernard?"

"I'm looking for him. Where is he?" he yelled.

"Sit down, Son."

"No. Where is he?"

"He was transferred early this morning."

Bernard's anger rose to a new level. He lost his one chance to avenge his brother's death.

"Why would you do that? You lied to my father. You said he was leaving tonight."

"I did. I lied once I saw the look in your father's eyes. I knew that either him or you would come for him, and that would be your only opportunity."

Bernard got closer to Olden. Maybe close enough for him to punch him or kick him or even shoot him. There was no telling where his pain would lead him. "Why would you protect him? You know what he did."

"Son, please calm down."

Bernard disobeyed; in fact, he grabbed Olden by the collar. "I needed to do this."

"I did it to protect you and your family. They wouldn't be able to live with a son being murdered and another son being in jail as a murderer. What would your family do without you? They already lost one son; they didn't need to lose another."

Bernard backed away, breathing hard and holding in tears. He knew Olden was right. His mind was so clouded with revenge that he didn't think about his family. All he could think about was George.

"Can I get you something to drink?"

"No, thank you." Bernard sat in the chair and started to calm down. "Sorry about this. You've done so much for our family."

"There's already been too much blood spilled in this small town. I just didn't want any more."

Those words stayed with Bernard on his drive back to his parents' house. He wanted to tell his dad that he made the right choice and that Olden might have just saved his life.

He rushed inside through the back door and noticed that the house seemed quieter than usual. He figured his parents were asleep. He thought he was right when he saw his mom laying still on the bed. But when his dad and the local doctor were next to her, he knew something was wrong. His dad's face was clammy and red, with puffy eyes filled with water. The doctor was packing his bag.

"Bernard?"

"Dad, what . . ." The rest of the sentence couldn't come out. He knelt on the other side of the bed. His mom lay there peacefully.

"Is she?" Bernard asked and received his answer when he touched her hand. He had never felt that type of cold before. He got on the bed and lay there crying beside his mom, refusing to believe it had happened. His dad held his hand for condolence, but mostly he was trying for bravery, trying not to let his tears spill out of his eyes. Bernard was crying so hard that it was hard for him to breathe.

There was no more rage, just pain and sorrow. Bernard thought of Ruben but not in the way he had earlier that day. Earlier, he had wanted him dead. Now he was actually glad he was put away for life. *He doesn't deserve death*, he thought. He should just sit in a cell for the rest of his life, embracing regret. Now he could no longer hurt his family. Ruben had done enough; because the moment he pulled the trigger, he didn't kill just one family member. That bullet killed two.

CHAPTER THIRTEEN

He tried as hard as anyone could, but Bernard couldn't muster up enough strength to throw the gun into the river. He stood on the edge of the Rio Grande a few days after his mom's death, still in shock by what happened. Even the doctor couldn't find a good enough diagnosis to explain her death. Bernard knew that the pain he felt for George's loss was worse for her; she had lost the will to live. That still didn't justify any of it. He lost both his mom and George within a week. Not only was George's funeral difficult to get through, but he knew that in one week, he had to be brave again and sit through his mother's funeral. He felt like his family would be wearing black for the rest of their lives. Sitting in the same church that everyone got married in, the same church that they went to every Sunday, the one he passed by on the way to work every day . . . now he would just think of it as the place for funerals.

He thought back to the week before everything happened, when everyone was sitting around the table at Whitey's laughing and congratulating George and Minnie. Now, Minnie won't even leave her house. Bernard heard they gave her a few days off from work, but she never went back. He planned to pay her a visit in the coming days. Mr. Soto had been over to her place, but only for a moment. He, too, couldn't bare showing his pain around others.

With all the hurt that had happened, there was still one thing left to be done. Bernard decided to walk to the river with the gun and chuck it. Not chuck it, but slam it into the water—an effort to try to throw his pain down with it. He envisioned it hitting the water, seeing a splash around the weapon, and then sinking to the ground, never to be found again.

So, he leaned back, and like throwing a baseball, he pitched it, only it never hit the water. It never left his hand. Something was holding him back. *There is so much bad history that comes with this gun,* he thought. *Why is it so difficult to get rid of this?* Bernard sat on the ground and listened to the river flow and the mosquitos buzz around him. He knew it wasn't the gun's fault. If he were to keep it, he would never be able to use it. Even holding it made the memories of the past few weeks worse.

He never knew his grandpa, the first owner of the gun, but his dad told him so many times how this gun was one of his greatest possessions. It wasn't the nicest or the sharpest, but it meant he would be safe whenever he needed to be. Bernard remembered times when his dad told him his grandpa used it to threaten drunks at the bar who tried to steal bottles or when he decided to finally get the initials engraved; he was so proud of it. His grandpa was described around town as a cowboy, nothing else to it. Just a cowboy in boots with spurs and this gun always strapped to him. He knew the stories that were told—that his great-grandparents came over with just sacks of clothes, a pair of shoes each, and a few coins, so when his grandpa made it to owning this bar and using this gun, he knew he couldn't be the one to do it.

Bernard wanted that feeling too. After his family passed away, what more could he ask for those remaining than to feel safe? He then thought he could always buy another gun and throw this one into the river. So, he decided that another gun would do. He stood up and swung his arm again. This time, the gun almost fell out of his palm, but his fingers brought it back. He came to his decision; he had to do something else with it.

The next night, extremely late, he brought a box, a hammer, and nails and walked out to the barn in the back of his house. Making his way past sleeping goats and sheep, he started pulling back the wooden paneling. While he most likely looked a bit insane, the process of yanking out rusted nails and ripping the barn walls off was helping him through the pain. Bernard didn't want the gun in the house, but he felt that letting it drown in the river—never to be used again—would be a disgrace to his dad and grandpa. He wanted it close enough that if Beto ever wished to have it, he would know where to get it, but it wouldn't be in a place where he would have to see it every day. After placing a few panels on the floor, Bernard pushed the slanted box in the wall between two supporting beams. He yelled. The animals were startled and moaned with annoyance. All his anger from the past few weeks came out. Sweat dripped from his face as he picked up the panels and hammered in the nails. He was almost done. With each stoke of the hammer hitting a nail into place, Bernard started to feel better. As if the nails driving in deeper covered his pain. Before he hammered it closed, he turned around to ensure that this spot would be a secret. Once it was all patched back up, he knew it would be for Beto someday, and he hoped he would never have to use it.

CHAPTER FOURTEEN

PART TWO

Forty-five years after Bernard hid the box for his son, Beto thought he might need it. He had had the weapon ever since his dad passed away, and he didn't feel comfortable leaving it hidden after they sold his parent's house. So, he kept it near, in the top dresser drawer, the one that had a lock on it, filled with bullets that were ready to protect.

Beto was in his late forties, with a wife, Maggie, and two boys of his own. Edward, the eldest, was in college in upstate New Mexico, and the other was Bernalillo's soon-to-be basketball star, Julian. The Soto boys looked a lot alike. They shared the same dark complexion as their father, but Julian was much taller. He was close to six foot two inches. He wasn't always the star player, though; that took time.

When Edward took off for school to study criminal justice, Julian could not deny that he was a little happy his older brother was leaving, though he would never admit to it. He was just entering high school and finally not living in his brother's footsteps. They went to the same school for most of their childhood, and Julian could have sworn his teachers never knew his name. Most of the time, the school faculty would call him "Edward's brother."

This year was going to be different. When the first day of freshman year came, he was completely ecstatic. He walked in with a stance that shined confidence. Little did he know that freshmen who walk in like that on the first day usually get bullied. And bullied he was. Nick Walton, a sophomore, one of the few pale, blond boys in their school, walked in with the same confident look. He made it seem like everyone was his friend, and those who weren't wanted to be. The girls blushed, and the guys gave him handshakes. It was a spectacle. So, when Julian walked in after him, Nick let him know there was only room for one popular guy. He picked Julian up over his shoulder and threw him butt-first into an open trash can during lunch. Julian was taller than his new enemy, but definitely not stronger. *How could this fifteen-year-old kid have muscles everywhere?* he thought. Julian mangled out of the trash can with a piece of half-eaten pizza dangling from his pants and yelled, "What the hell was that for?"

"Just putting you in your place, *Sombrero*." Nick smirked and laughed with his friends. Later, Julian noticed that was a name he called the Hispanic students.

Julian brushed it off and went back to an empty table to eat his lunch. He couldn't imagine a worse first day of school. He thought he was going to be the popular guy, but instead, he already had a bully. At least his classes would be fine, he hoped.

After the bell rang, he threw his trash in the large black can that he was sitting in a few minutes earlier and walked to his math class. He was always good at math, so he knew he would enjoy advanced algebra. Mr. Enriquez started to take roll. He called out a few names— Maria, Albert, somebody else that wasn't Julian. He was happy to see that his newfound bully wasn't in the same class. "Julian. Julian Soto," Mr. Enriquez called out.

"Here, sir."

"Soto? Oh, you must be Edward's brother!"

And there it was. Just a few hours in, and it was officially the worst first day of school. Since his brother didn't take advanced algebra, Julian assumed there would be no connection. What made it worse was that two more teachers after that noticed too. They told him how much they loved Edward.

Basketball was his last hope. It was the varsity team tryouts. He wasn't too confident, especially as a freshman, but he decided to go anyway. He went to the locker room early to change and get in a good warm-up before tryouts. Everyone was trying out, not just the freshman; that made Julian even more nervous. He had played all his life and was captain of his middle school team. He knew he was a good player, with a decent jump shot and excellent scoring total per game, but was that going to be enough?

A few players were already warming up on the court, throwing free throws and sprinting back and forth. Julian's nerves peaked so quickly that it was as if he pressed a button in his stomach. He decided to start out slow. He stretched, jogged around the court, and then did a few jump shots. He knew not to get too tired. More players showed up when the coach announced the drills. Julian moved fast from one side of the court to the other, dribbling the ball at a steady pace. He came close to the basket, jumped up, and threw the ball, which just barely touched the rim on its way in. The coaches asked to see two more drills. Those, too, were as easy as the first.

"It's time to pair off into mock teams. Shirts vs. Skins," Head Coach Monroe said. He called out the Skins first. "Peter, Nate, Rodrigo, Alfred, and Nick."

Julian quickly turned around. Coach Monroe did say it right. There, Nick, with a cocky face, stared straight at Julian. He didn't know how he missed him before now, but he guessed he was too focused during the drills. Even worse, Nick decided to try out for the same position. Julian always played best as a center so that's what he really wanted. The teams separated. Nick took his shirt off slowly, as if trying to impress someone, though Julian didn't know who.

When the game started, they were right on each other. Julian got the ball and moved toward the basket, but Nick distracted him. "Do you really think they will pick you, *Sombrero*? I played this spot all last year." Nick swung his arm down and took the ball right out of Julian's hands. The coaches were pleased. On the defense, Julian watched Nick's feet. They were quick, but his dribbling was slow. He noticed his patterns. He didn't think he could get the ball away, only if he did a jump shot. When he did and the ball went into the air, Julian jumped as high as he could and hit the ball to another shirt. "They might pick me now," he yelled and then smirked.

Nick looked pissed as the shirts scored again. Skins were winning, though, but only by two points. Coach Monroe called for a time-out. Julian drank water and watched Nick take some free throws. He was good. He made every one of them, but Julian still couldn't picture Nick as a basketball player. He was built and only about five foot eight, so Julian figured he would make more sense playing football. Their small-town high school had a better football team than basketball anyway. Julian couldn't imagine being on the same team and getting along.

They were back at it again. The teams were mixed up, but it was clear the coaches still wanted to determine who was the better center, so Julian and Nick remained opponents. "I'm open! I'm open," Julian yelled to the nearest player holding the ball. He quickly flung the ball to him. Julian ran for the basket and halted as Nick blocked his shot. He thought he could easily make it over him because of his height advantage. When he tried, Nick bumped his shoulder into him, making the ball slightly hover over the rim of the basket, but not making it in.

"Hey, that's a foul," Julian yelled.

While running back to the other side of the court, Nick yelled back, "Not here, it ain't. This is my court." From that point on, Nick gained even more confidence. The last part of the game was his. Nothing was blocking him. Julian was breathing hard, just trying to keep up. Nick must have made ten more points. He proved to everyone that it really was his court.

The next day, the list was posted on the gym door. Julian didn't feel confident, but he forced himself to go see anyway. He was surprised to see his name on the list. The coaches appointed starters. He wasn't on there, but Nick was. Julian didn't care; at least he made the team. Basketball meant the world to him, and this was his chance to prove his skills. He heard a voice behind him. "I guess I have to be nice to you now," Nick said as he turned around. Nick stuck out his hand, and Julian skeptically shook it. "Come on. Don't be like that. This will be fun."

Although Nick sounded sincere, Julian knew being around him would be anything but fun.

CHAPTER FIFTEEN

Julian could not have been more wrong. The bully turned out to be his best friend at school. Now that Edward was away, Nick was more than a best friend; he became another brother for Julian. They seemed inseparable. Nick often stayed the weekends at Julian's and picked him up every day for school. It was as if that handshake signified that he was going to stop being an ass. When basketball season came around, the two were basically attached at the hip. Well, not exactly, since Julian was so much taller. Nick was still a starter, and although that stung a little for Julian, he got a lot of playing time as a sub when Nick needed a break.

"So, are you gonna ask her out, or what?" Nick asked one day at lunch.

"What are you talking about?" Julian said, looking around the crowded cafeteria.

"The whole school can tell you have a thing for her."

"Dude, I can't. She's Coach's daughter."

"All the more reason. Look, if you don't, then I'm gonna do it for you."

Julian told him not to. He knew he was right. Isabella Monroe was one year older than Julian, but they were in the same math class. That's where he first saw her and mumbled some sort of hello. He wasn't sure he said hello at all. It was more of a grunt made by nerves. But she laughed and twisted her long, dark hair back behind her ear. It was that moment that Julian was determined to ask her out.

Sadly, it had been a month since that decision. No contact was made, not even a mumble—nothing. He was getting desperate. He was tired of hearing Nick talk about all the luck he gets with girls, so he went to the best guy he knew—his dad.

Beto was surprised when his son asked him for such a strange request.

"So, let me get this straight," Beto said to his son after dinner, "you want to take this girl to see the orchards?"

"Yeah, I thought that would be cool. She seems to like apples."

"How do you know?" Beto asked, squinting behind his glasses.

"Because she was eating one the other day at lunch."

Beto apologetically let out a big laugh. "So, just because she was eating an apple one day makes you believe she is an apple fanatic?"

"Sure. Why not?"

Julian's real plan was to show her how important his family was in their town. His grandfather, Bernard Soto, passed down a lot of properties to his family. Although they were not all thriving like they used to, his favorite was still the orchards. The orchards used to be open to the public, but after many years of people vandalizing the tress and picking their own apples without paying, the Soto family decided to fence them off. Now, only Beto and his sister Denny co-owned the property and had full access. So, that was Julian's plan. Take this girl there and show her how important they really were.

"Son, I'll let you, but under one condition."

"Sure, Dad."

"That you be responsible. Lock up after you go. Don't bother the workers if they are there. Don't take too many apples. Oh, and only take this one person."

That is definitely more than one condition, Julian thought, but he knew it best not to argue with his dad right now. They agreed with a handshake strong enough for a father and son. Julian's plan was almost perfect, except transportation. He decided that having his parents drive him, especially on the first date, would be too embarrassing. His brother, who was his second choice, was away, so he asked Nick. He had everything planned, expect for asking the big question. The next day, Nick said he would give them a lift, but he was a little skeptical when he learned that Julian hadn't even talked to Isabella yet. Luckily, that changed.

Julian was fortunate enough to be placed in a group assignment that day in their math class. They were given sheets with about fifteen equations to solve. The purpose of the assignment was for the groups to work together and talk through the problems. Julian's group, which had Isabella and a girl named Sophie in it, did the complete opposite. They each started to work in silence. It was almost becoming a competition to see who would finish first. After problem two, Isabella looked at Julian's and Sophie's papers to see which question they were on. Sophie was in the lead. After number three, Julian did the same. He was in second place. Not for long. Sophie finished number ten and looked at her teammates' papers. Julian was beating her. She let out an unexpected grunt and rushed to the next problem. Julian started laughing as he realized how ridiculous they were being. The rest of the class was acting like mature students who work well together, while these three nerds looked, well, nerdier.

"Ha. Finished!" Julian yelled.

The whole class looked at him like he had a horn growing out of his head, but Isabella didn't.

"Well, let's see if they are even correct," she said while she and Sophie checked his work.

"Not too bad, Soto, not too bad."

"You know my name?" he asked, thinking she didn't know he existed.

"Yeah, everyone knows you. Your brother is, um, Edward, right?"

Julian couldn't help but roll his eyes. "Yeah, that's him."

"He was in the same study hall as me last year. He always said that his little brother was going to be the next best basketball player here."

He didn't know which to believe more, his brother talking him up to pretty girls or this pretty girl talking to him. Julian could feel the excitement from actually speaking to his crush. It was all going so fast and so well that he didn't know what to say next, so, naturally, he blurted "Will you go out with me?"

Sophie laughed. "Wow, where did that come from?"

"Oh, I don't know. Forget I said anything."

"Sure, why not?" Isabella said after she noticed Julian's face was tomato-sauce red.

"How's tonight for you?"

Sophie laughed again. "Man, you sure don't waste any time."

Julian wanted to ask her to leave but thought it best not to seem as if he was trying too hard to impress this girl. Isabella agreed with a "cool" and a gentle smile. A few heartbeats later, Julian explained that his friend was going to give them a ride to someplace, but then he promised he'd scram. She seemed okay with all of it and excited for the surprise.

After the bell rang, she picked up her books and walked out with Sophie. They were probably talking about how awkward and forward he was. Julian watched her, which made him slightly worried about the night. But at least he did it. He wanted to throw up the entire time, but he did it, and to his surprise, she said yes. He officially felt like a real man.

Nick honked outside of Isabella's house that evening.

"Dude, I was gonna go to the door," Julian said.

"Oops, sorry, too late," he said, not seeming too sorry at all.

Isabella walked out with her dad, Coach Monroe. He walked her all the way to the car. Julian got out and opened the back door of Nick's Chevy Impala. Not the best car. Julian's dad's brand-new Pontiac Trans Am, what he called "the Bandit," would have been cooler, but this was his only choice. The Chevy's radio was always static, and most of the leather on the seats were ripped, so Nick hid them with blankets and sheepskin covers.

"Coach, nice to see you," Julian said and stuck out his hand.

Coach Monroe ignored it. "Yeah. Listen up you two. I expect you both to be gentlemen. The only reason I allowed this is because she begged for hours."

Isabella looked down, trying to pretend he didn't just say that. Coach Monroe placed his hand on the car. "If anything happens to her, I will destroy you. You will no longer exist."

Isabella pushed his shoulder. "Dad, stop please."

"Okay, have a nice time, dear, but seriously, boys, I mean it."

Isabella got into the car. And Coach Monroe turned to face both boys again. "I want her home before nine. No later."

Julian got in the car too, but a lot slower and with more fear. He had seen his coach angry and frustrated, but never threatening.

The drive over was quiet and somewhat awkward. Julian couldn't find the right words, and both Isabella and Nick were trying to make attempts at small talk, but nothing stuck. Julian let out a small sigh in relief once they made it.

"Thanks for driving us, man."

"Yeah, thanks. We'll see you later," Isabella said, almost upset that he had to take them.

"You know, I think I'll stick around." Nick said, "I've always wanted to see the famous Soto Orchards."

Julian grabbed Nick by the collar of his polo and pulled him closer so Isabella wouldn't hear. He asked him to leave and return when they were done, but Nick wasn't having any of it. He was determined to stay and hang around.

"Trust me, man, you won't even know I'm here." Nick smiled.

That was a lie. Not only was Julian breaking one of his dad's conditions, but his date was ruined. Julian tried to walk through the rows of trees with Isabella on his side, but Nick followed right behind them, interrupting by kicking up dirt and pulling on branches. Julian and Isabella continued walking through the rows, talking about school and doing their best to ignore Nick.

The few workers that were there when they arrived had already left. The sun was setting, which usually meant time to go home. Julian walked to the middle of the orchards and showed Isabella a small silver plaque on the ground in front of the largest tree there.

"This was the first tree that my great, great grandpa and his dad planted. There's a story in our family that my ancestors came here from a small town in Spain with just one pair of clothes and two coins. One of the coins was used to buy seeds for this tree."

"That's amazing, and it's still growing."

"Isabella," Nick blurted out, "I love the Sotos to death, but that story changes ever so slightly every time they tell it."

They both ignored him, so he came around the other side of the tree, stood on the tips of his toes, and grabbed an apple from the tree.

"Are you gonna pay for that?" Isabella asked.

"No, I don't think so. I get the friend's discount," he said with a wink and then took a large bite.

Julian rolled his eyes and looked down at the plaque. Both were ignoring the chomping sound coming from Nick. Isabella leaned over it. "What is the plaque for?"

Engraved in bold letters said: *In memory of George Soto. The strongest in our family.*

Julian took a deep breath. He didn't want to tell the entire story. It was a long one, so he just said, "When my dad was really little, his uncle passed away at a young age. This was put here to remember how brave he was."

Isabella wanted to ask what happened but couldn't because Nick took his immaturity to a new level. For no reason at all, he unzipped the fly of his jeans and pissed on the bottom of the tree.

"What the hell, *pendejo*?" Julian asked with disgust in his voice.

"What does that mean?"

Isabella shook her head. "You really are a dumbass."

"What? I had to go." Nick laughed. "Now the tree will grow twice as big."

Julian tried to brush it off, but Nick was purposely trying to ruin his time with Isabella. "Can you just go wait in the car?"

"Julian, it was just a joke," Nick said, trying to play it off. After they stared him down for a good minute, he decided to go to his car. Isabella and Julian started walking again. It was getting dark, especially because they were hiding from the sun in the trees, but he still wanted a few more minutes with her. He apologized for Nick's behavior.

She looked uncomfortable as if she had an itch on her arm. She explained, "Julian, there's something you need to know. I went out with Nick last year. Just once, and it didn't end well. He was a jerk the whole time and talked about how amazing his basketball game was. He didn't want to talk about anything else. Never once asked anything about me."

Julian looked at her. "I'm sorry to hear that. If I had known, I wouldn't have asked him to drive us."

"It's fine. I should've guessed it would be him. To be honest, I think he's a little envious."

"Why do you say that?"

"Well, two reasons. One, because I turned him down for a second date, and two, because even though he is here, I am having a really good time."

Julian blushed. It was dark, so he hoped Isabella couldn't tell. The sun was officially gone, so they started strolling to the car. It took ten minutes to walk back because they were deep in the orchards. They listened to their footsteps crushing leaves and brushing the ground.

Grasshoppers chirped alongside the faint sound of water from the distant Rio Grande. It was the right type of quiet—nature's quiet. Julian thought about how nice the date was. They walked side by side, taking turns glancing and smiling at each other. He then broke the sounds of nature. "I'll have my parents drive us next time."

"Please do," Isabella said with a soft smile.

They reached the front rows of trees, and Julian locked the gate behind them. He double-checked it was locked because he didn't want to break any more of his dad's rules.

"Hey, Julian," Isabella said with a crack in her voice.

He turned around and saw the reason for her tone. There was no car.

"Nick left us."

Julian felt the same anger that he did at the beginning of the school year when Nick stuffed him in the trashcan.

CHAPTER SIXTEEN

"I guess we should start walking back. Remember, I have to be back before nine," Isabella reminded with a shrug.

"No, no. I can't imagine anyone walking back that far, especially on a date."

Isabella softly laughed, still unsure what they were going to do. Julian jogged to the small adobe house on the side of the first row of trees. He used the same key to open the door. There, he dialed his home phone number onto the tan phone hanging on the wall. In no time, Beto was there to pick up his son.

"*Mijo,* what happened?"

"Dad, thank you. This is Isabella."

She said hi and politely thanked him as she slouched to get into the back seat of the Bandit.

"How did you guys get here?"

"Nick brought us, but I asked him to go back to the car, and I know I was only supposed to bring one person, and I'm sorry. I learned my lesson now. Anyway, he got mad and left us."

"Well, I have to wonder why he left. He must've had some reason."

Over the past few months, Beto had not only come to like Nick, but he also had sympathy for him. He always hung around their house. On many nights, he stayed the night in Edward's old room. He was polite and helpful, so Beto thought there must be more to the story. As for Julian, he was surprised that his dad wasn't mad, but he knew they would talk about it later.

On the way back home, Isabella and Julian talked as if his dad wasn't even there. She told him to talk with Nick at school the next day and tell him what he did was wrong.

Julian tried to do just that, but Nick beat him to it with an apology. Apologizing wasn't his style, but he did it well. He said he never should have acted that way, and he would pay for the apples. He felt guilty about leaving them and still thought they walked back to town.

"Your feet must be killing you, man. I'm sorry," Nick said while touching Julian's back.

Julian decided to go with it. "Yeah, they are. Isabella almost twisted an ankle."

A look of pity struck his face, which made Julian smirk. They made their way to the school gym for practice.

"Is there anything else you want to tell me?" Julian hinted.

"Well, now that you mention it, I took more apples before I left."

That wasn't what Julian was getting at. He wanted Nick to confess about his date with Isabella. Julian assumed the only reason Nick suggested he ask her out was because he wanted to see if she would turn him down too. Turns out, his assumption was right.

"I'm just surprised she didn't turn you down. She's known for that, dude."

"Nope, she even agreed to a second date."

"Well, that's cool, man."

Things got worse for Nick that day. Coach Monroe announced the new starters for the next game. The team huddled around to listen.

Nick's name didn't come up; instead, Julian was starting.

"Coach," Nick interrupted, "was there a mistake? There are only two more games left."

"There was no mistake."

Julian tried to hide his excitement. It felt like his heart wanted to jump out of his chest. It took everything in him not to start running around the gym. He didn't know that Coach Monroe was watching him so much. He was trying his best at every practice, he stayed after to work on his jump shots, and his game seemed to be improving. Especially being a freshman, he knew he needed to prove his hard work in the next game.

Nick couldn't let it go. "Coach, come on. We should finish out the season strong."

"I would like that too. That's why I made a new starting list."

"You did, or your daughter did?"

The whole team and coaching staff got quiet. No one knew what he intended except for Julian, Coach Monroe, and Nick. Coach Monroe asked to speak to him privately.

No one knew what happened during that meeting, but at the next game, Nick wished Julian good luck. It was surprisingly sincere. In fact, Nick seemed supportive and understanding the whole game.

The game was coming to a close, and the team was down by one point. Since it was one of the last few games, the bleachers were packed with family and friends. Julian had been playing a steady game. Nick subbed for him once, only for two minutes before halftime. After the half, Julian took over with more speed than he knew he had. Once he got hold of the ball, he ran and dodged the opposing team members faster than he thought he could. He was no longer slower than others, and he was finally using his height to his advantage.

Maybe it was his newfound confidence as a starter or the fact that, as a freshman, he had a sophomore girlfriend and new friends and was doing well in his classes, but he was determined to show off to everyone. And so he did. The team caught up to only one point behind and only a few seconds on the board. The only problem was they didn't have the ball. Julian knew he needed to steal to score. He focused on number four. His footwork was slow while dribbling, so once number four got the ball, Julian knew exactly how to get it away from him. Luckily, they passed to number four. Since he was a bit slower, Julian quickly left the player he was blocking and ran to him, which wasn't part of Coach's play. He blocked his pass and jumped to grab the ball. He grasped it by the tips of his fingers and used his speed to make the winning shot.

That game was the start of Julian's successful basketball career. For the next two years, he was unstoppable. At that moment, the bleachers showed a sea of people screaming and clapping their hands. Julian looked at his team. The entire row of players jumped up cheering, except for one. Nick sat still. He was slowly clapping and somewhat smiling, but his demeanor was different from his teammates. Julian tried to assure himself that this wouldn't change a thing—they were still best friends.

CHAPTER SEVENTEEN

"You know what's more cutthroat than the presidential election?" Maggie asked Julian, then abruptly said, "Small-town elections."

"Why are you even watching this, Mom?"

"Because they are so entertaining," she told Julian as she turned the volume up on their box TV. For the past thirty minutes, she had been on the edge of the sofa, glued to the news station covering the upcoming elections. She was particularly interested in the county sheriff. Since the previous sheriff's term was up, two newcomers were running.

"Come on, take a seat," Maggie said, patting the other side of their sofa.

Julian slumped down on the cushion, wishing to do anything else with his weekend. Maggie was always interested in the town's news. Not just the news but the gossip too. Everyone else in the family did not seem to care. She started clapping while keeping her eyes glued to the TV, seeming like she was watching a professional sports team play a championship game.

"They say he's up. He will probably be projected to win by next week."

Julian rolled his eyes. "Is there anything else on?"

"Oh, come on. Don't you want to hear his speech?"

"Who? That one." Julian pointed to the older candidate on the screen.

"No, that's Johnson. He is most likely to lose. No, I'm betting on Castro." She pointed to the younger man. He was slightly taller with a darker complexion and a chunky, dark mustache.

"Why him?" Julian asked with mild curiosity.

"I'm not too sure. There is something about him. It doesn't even matter about the party he is running in. I just think there's something there."

"Like what?"

Maggie cleared her throat. "No one has ever heard of him. Even though he comes from upstate, I think he can bring something to our little town. I think he and the mayor can save us from our situation too."

Julian vaguely knew of the situation she was talking about. He had overhead many of his parents' conversations about the businesses, but he never paid much attention. He was probably too focused on the next game or going out with Isabella, but for some reason, the businesses, expect for the bar, were just not making it like when his grandfather or even great-grandfather ran them. He recalled the most recent time his parents sat at the kitchen table looking at stacks of bills and receipts, their faces nowhere near happy.

The news focused on a clip of Castro's most recent speech. He stood at a podium at the latest town street fair. The crowd wasn't large, but there was no denying their engagement.

"That's what we need." Castro paused. "We need safety. We need security. No one should be afraid to let their kids walk to school. No one should be afraid to walk to dinner at night without getting mugged. These are some of the things this town has been seeing. Now, I know what you are thinking. I'm not native to your wonderful town, but I got here as soon as I could. The small-town feel is something people dream of having. I mean, we have the best of both worlds—a big city that is twenty minutes away, but we have less traffic, people who actually wave hello, and way better food."

The crowd laughed. Maggie said, "See, that's why he will win. No one knows about his past. Johnson has been in this town forever. Everyone knows what he did as a teenager."

Castro continued, "So, let's get out there and vote next week. Most of this town feels safe in their own neighborhood, but we need to keep it that way."

The sound of the back door shut and the only thing to pull Maggie's attention away from the screen was the sound of muddy boots hitting the kitchen floor.

"What do you think you're doing, Beto? You know you need to leave those outside."

Beto gave an eye roll and a slight huff, then stated, "Of course, *mi amor*."

"Don't think I didn't see that," Maggie yelled and turned her head back to the TV.

"I promise to hire more staff and officers," Castro continued with a slight stroke of his mustache. "I promise to keep the scheduled patrol, and I promise I will personally see to the law and order that we need. I am the type of person who cannot stand for injustice."

Castro placed his hands on the podium as if he was running miles and needed to take a breath. He continued, but his voice became deeper and slower.

"Have you ever felt that someone did you wrong? Have you ever felt that someone walked all over you as if you or even your family were little bugs they could kill? That is not okay with me. We should never feel like we are peasants to a king. That has happened to me, and I didn't stand up when I could. I am here to stand up now. I am here to stand up for that oppression. I am here to stand up for you. Thank you."

Castro finished with a smile and waves as the crowd clapped and cheered. He gave one last nod and made his exit from the podium.

"See, that's it."

"What?" Julian asked his mom.

"I can tell he wants it," she said, still staring straight at the screen.

Julian squished his eyebrows together. "Wants what? You mean to win?"

"No, justice."

CHAPTER EIGHTEEN

Nick had been a senior for over half a semester and was eager to get a basketball scholarship. But when the college scouts came to watch their game, they were more interested in Julian. Even though Julian got most of the playing time, the two remained good friends.

It was early spring, and Julian had noticed that Nick was having a hard couple of months, maybe even years. He was not the same guy he had met two years before. He still held some popularity, but only because he was close to Julian.

Nick's mother passed away from cancer when he was a kid, and his father was always hard on him. Julian assumed Nick's father secretly and unfairly took his wife's death out on his son. The number of nights that Nick asked to spend in Edward's room was increasing. "His dad was in one of his moods"—this was the usual excuse, but Julian figured out that Nick's dad didn't just get moods; he got violent.

Nick gave sad excuses—he had black eyes because he ran into a door or was clumsy and fell while working on his car. Julian brushed them off, but he knew where those bruises originated. It got to the point where the Soto's expected Nick there every weekend. Julian's parents didn't mind; they appreciated his kindness and willingness to help around the house. He was thankful that Julian's mom always had enough food, so the teenagers were rarely hungry.

"Man, if your mom keeps making tamales like those, I'm gonna have to move in," Nick said jokingly as he was planning on going home that night.

"I'm sure they wouldn't mind, dude, but is everything okay at home?" Julian stabbed at the truth.

"It's fine, man. I told you my dad just gets upset and wants to be alone some nights. That's all."

Julian was going to take another jab, but he didn't have time. Nick was already in his car, ready to leave this conversation behind.

"Hey," he yelled as he started the engine, "will you remember to ask your dad for me?"

"Yeah, no problem. I'll ask him once I get inside."

Nick waved goodbye and sped out of the driveway. When Julian got inside, he joined his dad on the sofa in front of the TV. He was at the beginning of an episode of *MASH* when Julian interrupted.

"Hey, Dad, I was wondering if I could ask you for a favor."

"Sure, *mijo*," he said while lowering the volume on the TV.

"Well, you know Nick is going through a lot. I was wondering if you had a job open at the bar, just as a barback or busboy. He just needs to start saving some money."

"Is he planning on paying us rent?"

Julian figured that was a joke, but just in case, he asked, "I thought you guys were cool with him crashing here?"

"Of course we are, but why does he need the job so bad?"

"He said it was for college. To be honest, he has had no luck getting a scholarship," Julian said, feeling a little guilty. If Nick was put in the game more often, the scouts might be more interested, but Coach Monroe kept playing Julian. He even asked Coach to put in Nick for the majority of the last home game, but Coach shrugged him off. Coach Monroe was determined to get the team to a higher scoring average, and playing Julian was the only way to get there.

"I understand, Son. Tell Nick to come in for an interview tomorrow after school. We might have something for him."

Julian felt relieved. Finally, something good would happen for his friend. He couldn't wait to tell him.

The next night, Nick told Julian over the phone that his dad is tough during interviews.

"Your dad wanted to know if I had a résumé, work experience, even references. I told him no, that this would be my first job. He didn't look impressed, but I got the job. I'll be a barback, and since I am eighteen, I can start mixing drinks and serving them. He said I'll make pretty good tips if I do good."

Julian said, "That's great, dude. When do you start?"

"Tomorrow. Your dad said he will work around practice and our games, but it could eventually be a full-time deal once the summer starts."

Nick was more than excited, and he showed it in his work. To everyone's surprise, he was a hard worker. He was trained quickly. He started taking orders and serving at the bar that same day. He stayed late on most days and even went back to reclean certain areas.

The regulars at the bar were skeptical. "Who's the kid?" many of them kept asking while nursing their drinks, but Nick, the charmer, won them over. He would greet them at the door and have their drinks ready by the time they sat down. Even Beto was shocked by how good he was.

After months of working after school and weekends at less than minimum wage, Beto decided that Nick deserved a few more dollars a day. Beto called him into the office one day.

"Mr. Soto, I am surprised. Are you sure?" Nick asked.

"I am. I know you're saving for school."

"Thank you. I could really use it."

Nick waited as Beto reached into a drawer to get his ledger to change Nick's payment and get it re-signed. Nick looked around the room. No one was ever in the office except for Beto. In fact, it was kind of a mess. Papers on the floor, the file cabinet stuffed full, and a thick layer of dust over mostly everything, especially the painting on the wall.

Everyone knew the history of the bar and their family, and everyone knew that ever since then, the safe had yet to be used. Nick was sure the family's money was put in a real bank, and the safe was shut for good. He knew all these rumors, of course. Everyone did. In fact, it was folklore, some story that families around town liked to tell on holidays. Some people still think that the money was never moved. That it is all still there, and even more is added. Everyone assumed there would be enough to feed the town for a few months. Nick never gave in to the rumors, even when kids at school asked him about it. He didn't bother with the gossip.

Nick signed the agreement for his new paycheck and sincerely thanked his best friend's dad once again. He started for the door when Beto asked him one thing.

"Nick, do you know what we always say in our family?"

"I'm not sure, sir."

"We say family comes first."

Nick slowly blinked and nodded, remembering Julian saying that once or twice.

"I am only telling you this, Son, because, well, you have been like family to us. I know your life at home isn't the best, so if you ever need anything, we are here for you," Beto said sincerely and calmly.

"Thank you, Mr. Soto. You are right. Life at home isn't the best. My dad is"—he paused, not sure what to say—"well, thank you. It's an honor to be welcomed into yours."

Beto waved goodbye with a smile as Nick left the office. He watched what felt like his third son leave the bar. Little did he know that he would betray the entire Soto family only a week later.

CHAPTER NINETEEN

"We just need a nice cake," Maggie said on the phone.

"Why do I have to go get it?" Beto grunted as he asked.

"Because you're right down the street. I want to have a cake for tonight."

Beto agreed to run by the bakery on his way home. Later that evening, the family was getting together for Nick's graduation party. He entered the crowded bakery, which worsened his mood. While standing in line, he saw a few familiar faces, though many others he had never seen before. He looked at the selection of ready-made cakes and tried to decide on the right one. He wondered why Maggie couldn't just make one herself. He then figured she would be busy making all the other food. He couldn't believe she invited over thirty people. She knew he didn't really like being around large groups. He would be happy just having dinner with Maggie and the boys.

"That's him. He is a part of *that* family in town," whispered a lady to another one behind him. Both women were small with white hair and wore bulky cardigans despite the warm weather.

"The one they say owns everything in town?"

"They don't own *everything*, and they shouldn't own *anything*. They did shady things back in the day to keep it all running."

Beto held his tongue and pressed his lips together. *What's the use of arguing in line with abuelas who just want to gossip?* he thought. He knew they enjoyed talking about the town's people, but he wondered why they had to speak so loudly. He assumed, *Gossiping gets louder the older you get.*

"That's probably why you said you never see him out." The second lady spoke again, trying to lower her volume. Others in line started to turn around.

"If they weren't thieves, they wouldn't have any of these businesses."

That was it. Beto started to turn around, but another woman, who was slightly younger, jumped in. "Shirley, dear, I see you every day at that grocery store, and your son is a regular at the bar, so maybe we should be grateful that we have local family businesses. Small businesses are harder to keep these days."

Shirley and her friend stopped chatting and gave multiple side-eyes to everyone. Beto made his cake choice, paid, and left. He wondered if he should say something on the way out—to the younger lady or the ones spreading rumors—but he decided against it. It took everything in him not to defend his family, but he wondered if there was some truth to their words.

He knew rumors had spread ever since the Soto family came to New Mexico. Most of the gossip about the bootlegging and gambling rooms were true, and although it was helpful to the family through those many years, it was technically illegal. He knew the gossip didn't stop there. Over the years, the rumors grew, and the family turned into thieves and murderers, really anything to help people stay entertained. Though it wasn't everyone. The family did have many alliances in town, especially those they didn't even know, like that very woman in line that stopped Shirley's gossip.

That younger woman had truth in her words too. Their small businesses were not going to make it forever. Beto could see it every day, especially with the new mayor and other city officials. Although he didn't watch politics for sport like his wife, he could see that they were doing the opposite of what he hoped. The family noticed city officials were trying to make this a big city when this was always meant to be a small town.

The sun was starting to fade, and Maggie became frantic. She was running around yelling out orders to Beto and the boys. She had been cleaning the house for the past week. Beto noticed some cars pulling up in their driveway. Now, Beto was no doubt a grumpy old man, but when a party was happening, he turned into a ringman in a circus. Julian was always shocked and somewhat impressed at his quick personality change.

"Hola, *amigos!*" he kept yelling as he was offering drinks and sitting people at tables in their backyard. He even turned up the music on their stereo multiple times. He was only one drink in but acting as if he owned the world. *Maybe this personality change fueled the town's rumors*, he thought.

Denny wrapped an arm around Beto. "Careful, *hermano,* or people are going to think you're actually having a good time."

Beto shrugged off her arm and comment. "I think I deserve it every once and a while."

"I would agree. I like this side of Beto, better than the boring senior citizen who worries about everything."

"Well, I can't live my life like a constant party like you do."

Denny flipped her short hair behind her ear and said, "Maybe you should give it a try."

Beto responded with silence. She understood what her brother was going through. As a co-owner of one of the businesses, she was helping as much as possible, but she also had a career that she loved. The businesses were disintegrating, but her passion was teaching and working with children. She wanted to spend her time in a classroom and not worry about businesses that were forced onto them. Often, she wished that Beto did not have to go through this, as if he never took over the properties, but it's hard to say no when it's an inheritance.

"Seriously, though, if you have to close down the other businesses, then just do it. It's not worth all the stress, and we all know you'll still have the bar. Your one true baby."

"Try telling that to Dad or even Granddad."

"I can't because they are not here anymore. Beto, stop living like they are sitting on your shoulder, watching your every move. They never had to deal with what you are going through. We are living in a different time. It will be tough, like losing a loved one, but it is for the best."

Beto nodded. He knew deep down what he had to do, but completing the task could kill him. Denny placed a hand on his shoulder. "What would they do if they were living now?"

Beto took in a short sip of his drink. He saw some of his neighbors coming up to him and realized their conversation was about to end. Before he moved, he turned back to his sister and said, "They would put family first."

People ate and congratulated Nick. Somehow, the invite list doubled. There were friends from school, but mostly people around Beto and Maggie's age.

"Hey, dude, who are all these people?" Nick asked while pulling Julian aside.

Julian scanned the backyard. "I think most of them are my cousins?"

"You don't know all your cousins?"

"No, not really. It's a Mexican thing."

The two laughed and started for the cake. Even though Nick did not know these people, he was happy to be surrounded by those who wanted to come. Maybe they came for the food, but at least he was part of it. He got a few graduation gifts. Most were cards with a few dollars, but he was more than okay with that. He kept looking the whole night; no, his dad never showed. Nick knew he was sitting at home all day in his recliner and going through beer cans.

"Congratulations, man," Julian said as they finished their slices of cake.

"Thanks. This was cool of your parents to do."

"Yeah, sorry there's not too many younger people."

Nick smirked. "Don't worry. I've got a plan for that next weekend."

CHAPTER TWENTY

Nick had plans to make it the ultimate party. The school year just ended, and he wanted to go out with a bang. So, since his dad would be out of town, he thought throwing a party in his backyard by the shed would be perfect. He went with it even though he thought it might be too small to fit the entire junior and senior classes. Options were limited.

He started by telling a few friends at school. Unfortunately, they didn't seem interested. Nick knew that every upperclassman would appear if he told Julian and Julian spread the word. He was jealous but knew it would be the only way to get people there. He wanted this party to be what he was remembered for. He wanted to be the guy who threw the best end-of-the-year party. Ever since he lost the most popular jock spot to Julian, he was determined to get it back.

So, a few days before the party, he asked Julian, "Would you mind spreading the word? Next weekend. Nine o'clock. Only upperclassman. Oh, and of course, only those who won't rat us out."

"What about booze? People aren't going to come if you don't

have alcohol."

Nick knew Julian was right. He had completely forgotten that teenagers only want to stand around and drink at parties. He originally figured Julian's influence would be enough, but he knew he needed both. To avoid looking like an amateur, he lied and said, "I've got it all under control." Julian nodded with skepticism on his face.

Later that day, the school was buzzing with excitement for the weekend. Only one thing was wrong. Everyone was calling it "Julian and Nick's party." *They could have at least put my name first*, Nick thought.

He needed to fix that. Julian still had another year at school, while Nick desperately wanted to leave a legacy. He wanted next year's seniors to talk about him even though he was gone. He knew there was only one thing that would make it right. Lots of alcohol. If everyone knew that he provided the location and drinks, then there would be no doubt that it was his party and only his.

He thought of every plan possible. He had $150 saved and wasn't stupid enough to spend it all on booze. He knew he needed that for school. His dad was always drinking, which is what probably fueled his anger toward him. After checking each hiding place, even underneath his dad's bed, all he could find were empty bottles and a couple packs of cigars. *He probably drank all of this week's paycheck*, he thought. He started to get frustrated. *It isn't fair. I shouldn't have to spend all my hard-earned money. Maybe just half. . . . No. I worked too hard for that.*

That's when desperation fueled stupidity, which took on a whole new form. He created a plan for how he would get enough booze and how it would work out in his favor, or so he thought. He was going to steal from work.

The party meant a great deal to him because while stealing the alcohol, he felt an overwhelming sense of guilt. Although it was starting to make him feel sick, he didn't stop.

Nick was hired to close the bar that night, which meant he would do all the cleanup. At this point, Beto's trust in Nick grew because he gave him a key to the bar for closing. Beto told him that only family members were ever given a key to the bar. This is what made his plan feel even more disgraceful. He was letting down the people who had been so kind to him.

Again, nothing stopped him from grabbing bottles off the top shelf. He took down a few bottles of vodka, rum, and whiskey. He knew if the bottles went completely missing, someone would notice, so he poured the alcohol into his own pitchers from home and poured in water and iced tea to make it look like they were never even touched. He knew those bottles would not get used for a while. The main bartenders used the bottles on the top last, which was where he stole from. He would make sure to go back and hide those bottles another night when he had more time. Carefully, he placed them back without removing the thin layer of dust on the shelf.

It worked, he thought while locking up. He took the amount of six large bottles of alcohol. After loading his car, he slowly drove home, trying not to spill the pitchers, and got ready for his big night. Sliding on his best button-down shirt and cleanest jeans, he felt ready for the evening and not concerned about his earlier actions.

At nine o'clock, no one was there. Nick started to panic. He had gone through all of this, even possibly lost his job, for no one to show up. When a few people pulled into the driveway and walked around the back, they asked for two things. One, "Where is the booze?" And two, "Where's Julian? I thought this was more his party?"

Nick started to get angry. Did people really not like him, or did they only like him because of Julian? He quickly corrected them and handed them a red plastic cup. He became a thief all to have everyone think this was Julian's idea. When Julian showed up with Isabella, that's when the party felt like it started. Nick got recognition from a few people. A few high fives and "nice party, dude," but it was not what he wanted. He imagined everyone noticing him, even putting him on their shoulders, but instead, he started drinking the stolen alcohol—a lot of it. He hoped that getting alcohol in his system would make this night better.

"Dude, maybe you should slow down. You've taken, what, ten or eleven shots of that?" Julian asked.

Nick pushed him away and started toward the shed. To make the night memorable, the last thing to try was to bring out his dad's motorcycle. *After everyone gets a look at the blued-stripped Harley*, he thought, *there is no way they will forget this night*. It was late, and a few people left to make their curfew. Nick was persistent, willing to give up everything for one night.

He stumbled his way over to the shed. He overheard Isabella with a group of friends. They formed the perfect circle a few feet away and talked about college. Even through blurred vision, he could make out Isabella, Sophie, and at least two other girls from the debate team.

"Are you really planning on going out of state?" one girl in the group asked Isabella.

"Arizona State is not that far."

"But why did you choose there?" another girl asked.

Nick slowed down just to hear more. The girls didn't see him lurking.

"That's where Julian plans to go. Don't say anything yet, but they were talking about giving him a full scholarship for basketball."

"That would be so good for you two. You can continue dating in college," another said.

Nick made a list in his drunken state. Julian got the girl, then the starting spot on the team, and then popularity. Not only does he have the perfect family, but now he is going to get a full ride. This list added gasoline to the fire. While his anger increased, his last hope was the bike. As he stormed into the shed, he turned the key over and tried to start up the bike, all to find out that his dad left it sitting there on empty. He thought again, *Even if I did show them the bike, it would not be nearly as fascinating as Julian's life.*

He got dizzy, mostly because of all the whiskey. He decided he needed a new plan—a new shot at being remembered. He looked around in his dad's dusty old shed. There was nothing but yard tools, car parts, and a worthless bike.

That's when he thought of something—something that was created from jealousy and mixed with hatred and alcohol. He rose to his feet while almost throwing up all the liquor in his system, grabbed the axe off the wall, and started making his way toward Julian.

CHAPTER TWENTY-ONE

As fast as a heartbeat, the backyard cleared with one shot from a gun. *Who in the world brought a gun,* Nick questioned? The sound made him jump, but it didn't stop his raging thoughts. Cars were pulling out of the driveway. Teenagers were running home. He was in such a drunken state of anger and frustration that he couldn't think about someone shooting; all he could think about was hurting Julian.

Nick found him standing alone. Axe in hand, ready to be used, he was breathing heavy with bright, red eyes.

"Hey, man. I'm sorry. It must have been my fault. I told him I was here. I don't know why he did that."

Nick had no idea what he was talking about. All he could think about was how much he hated his friend.

"You took everything I ever wanted," Nick yelled. "You had it all. Why did you need more?"

"What are you talking about? Is this about my dad?"

Nick raised the axe and slurred, "What do you mean, your dad?"

"He just got here. He told everyone to leave, and when that didn't work, he shot in the air. Is this why you're mad?"

"Of course he did. Always looking out for his little *mijo*," Nick said, closing the space between them.

"Nick, you're drunk. You need to go to bed."

Julian tried to pass him, but Nick stepped in his way, still raising the axe.

"Get out of my way, you idiot."

"Take one more step, and this axe falls on your neck, *Sombrero*."

Julian noticed he wasn't kidding. It was a long time since he heard that name. He could see how red his face was. The fire in his eyes. He knew that if he said or did anything else, Nick might actually go through with it. The axe was right above his head, with the edge facing downward. Julian couldn't move. He was too afraid to. He wondered what he did to bring Nick to this point. Wondering didn't matter much. Nick had his life in his hands.

"Drop the axe," Beto said firmly.

Nick didn't move. He saw out of the corner of his eye that Beto was a few feet behind him. He knew he was around here somewhere. He also saw what he was holding. In Beto's hand was a silver gun with a wooden handle pointed right at his head.

"Drop it, boy. I mean it."

"You won't shoot me," Nick said, facing Julian. They were standing in a perfect line. Beto was behind Nick. Nick was in front of Julian. It was only a matter of seconds before someone stepped out of line.

"If you hurt my son, that will be the last thing you ever do."

Julian didn't move. He was thinking of a way out. "You still wouldn't do that to me."

"You have been around us enough to know that I can shoot you, and no one would blink an eye."

Nick knew it was probably true. He looked at Julian with so much hatred. Julian realized then that he would have done it if his dad weren't there. Nick got an idea and went with it. He threw the axe backward in Beto's direction. The spiraling axe made Beto leap out of the way and avoid getting hit. When he did, he accidentally dropped his most precious item.

The boys looked at the gun. It was as if the world stopped spinning. Although it was dark, they could see two letters shining up from the side of the gun—G.S.

Julian had never seen the gun in person. Although he had heard the story many times, his dad kept it hidden. He got one more look at it lying on the floor before Nick grabbed it.

Everything happened so fast. Beto tried to grab the gun from Nick but failed as he shoved him back. Julian stayed as still as he could while Nick pointed the gun at him. Nick had never shot a gun before. When he did, he missed Julian's head, but the bullet hit his forearm.

Blood came out in a long, steady stream. Julian called for his dad in agony while using his other hand to cover up the wound. Nick slowly stepped back in shock. He placed the gun on the ground and made a run for it. Beto and Julian raced to the Bandit and headed straight for the hospital, leaving Nick shaking and hiding in the trees. He remained there, staring at the revolver that was lying in the dirt.

"Your basketball career is over," said the doctor about three days after the shooting. Julian and his dad had gone in for his final appointment.

The doctor said, "There is too much damage to your radius bone. We tried everything we could to repair the muscle around it, but if you are looking to play basketball in the next couple of years, I think it would be impossible. It is going to be very difficult for you to twist and turn your forearm like you used to. The bullet went through all the good tissue, and as much as we tried, it won't repair like new. Hopefully, it will return to new in a few years."

Years? Julian questioned. He acted tough, but hearing that he would not be able to play basketball like he used to was almost as painful as being shot in the arm. His emotions felt like a simmering pot. Not only were his future goals ruined, but his best friend in the entire world betrayed his family and almost killed him.

"Leave the cast on for the next two months, and then I'll see you back here. Then we can talk about physical therapy."

After the doctor left, two police detectives waited outside the door.

"Dad," Julian said, "before they come in, can I ask for a favor?"

"Yes."

"Just don't tell them who did it."

"No. I am putting that boy in jail. He stole from our family. If I hadn't gone to do inventory that night, I would have never found him at that party. And where would you have been? You would have been dead."

"I get that, Dad, but why would you bring the gun in the first place? You could have just shown up and confronted or threatened him and never shot it."

"Anger is not the best quality in this family, especially when someone takes what isn't theirs."

Julian knew that, but he felt differently. It was as if that gene was not passed to him. Or as if his emotions would always be simmering and never boil over. Maybe it took time. Maybe over the years, it would start to develop, but looking at his dad's state the other night, seeing the rage in his eyes just because of a few bottles, he secretly hoped it never would.

Julian adjusted his position in the hospital bed. "Dad, please. I know it doesn't make sense, but please. He was in a bad place. He felt like I took everything away from him."

Beto was not surprised. Julian was always looking out for everyone else. In some strange way, he was sure Julian thought this was partly his fault too.

"I don't think I can just let him get off without anything."

"He's gone. He left town. Isabella said his dad was looking for him around Main Street. I'm sure he is gone for good. You'll never see him again. Please, Dad, do me this one favor."

Beto nodded slightly.

"No, I need you to promise."

"I promise," Beto mumbled slowly.

After he agreed, he thought of something else, something equally important. "I need to speak to the police officers about one thing. Is that still okay?"

Julian nodded. He had an idea of what his dad wanted.

Beto walked out the door and into the waiting room. He spoke quietly, even though it was just the two detectives and him in the room.

"*Beinvenidos*, officers. We have decided to call off the case. We no longer want to pursue the crime. I am sorry we wasted your time." He was gritting his teeth through every word. His promise to his son was more important.

One said, "Are you sure, Mr. Soto?"

"Yes, everything is fine." The words tasted like vinegar to him.

The officers wrote down their new orders on their notepads, each doing brief, small scribbles.

"I need one thing from you all. I need to get my gun back. Do you know where it is?"

The two gentlemen looked at each other. One said in a hurry, "We went to the residence where you said the incident happened, and we couldn't find a weapon. We looked everywhere. We even searched the house. I'm sorry, sir, but it's gone."

CHAPTER TWENTY-TWO

After that night, things crumbled for Beto and his family. Over the next year, Beto had to close the grocery store and the apple orchard business. Two of the three businesses passed down to him were no longer making ends meet. Ever since the Walmart and Target moved into their small town, there was no need for a local grocery store with half of what those stores were providing. Locals were more than happy to drive a little bit further for a name-brand store.

It was around the same time that the apple orchards were not worth the time and cost either. Stores were buying apples in larger supplies, delivered on eighteen-wheelers. After they let all the workers go, people were not willing to pick through the trees themselves. That became old quickly. In fact, it was only something people enjoyed doing during the fall.

It almost killed him, laying off all the workers and closing the doors for good. It became hard for Beto to look himself in the mirror. His family worked so hard for years, and when it came down to it, he was the one who couldn't withstand the future and its changes. His father and grandfathers all made it work, but he, in the line of the Soto men, failed. On top of all that, he continued to think about his actions the night of Nick's party—storming in with a loaded weapon and then leaving that weapon only to never see it again. The feeling of losing everything, especially the small family history, weighed him down. His everyday actions became difficult to achieve, with guilt and depression at every step.

Foolish mistakes, he often told himself. He should have been thinking of more ways to keep the businesses going. He knew they would start to feel the cut in money, especially now that Julian was going to college in about a month.

Little did he know, he wasn't the only one in town having money troubles. In fact, financial problems led to Nick's father's actions the night of his son's party. Beto always wondered what happened between them. It must have been something bad for him to leave town. It could not have been the shooting that made him leave. He rarely saw Nick's father, and the few times he did, he quickly looked away and ignored Beto. He wished he knew what happened, but the only people who knew the full story were Nick's father and Sheriff Castro.

When Nick's father walked into the house that evening, his son was passed out on their sofa. The backyard was filled with paper cups and a few empty glass bottles. Their gates were open, and the living room and kitchen lights were on.

Since his current job as a truck driver was not lucrative enough, he was out of town searching for a job upstate. Although he didn't want to admit it, he was about to get fired. After pleading with his boss, his boss said he needed to pay back the stolen money from the register.

A few weeks prior, he stole a couple hundred. He considered it an early paycheck. Even after he muddled through an apology, his boss didn't care. He had one week to come up with the money. He wasn't going to get it. Every job prospect up north didn't want him. So, when he came home to remanence of a party, he slapped his son on the back.

"Get up, boy."

Nick slid off the sofa and onto his feet in a groggy state. "What? What happened?"

"Go clean up all your shit outside. What the hell were you thinking?"

Nick started coming to reality and took three or four steps away from his dad.

"You think just because I'm gone, you get to pull something like this?"

"I wasn't thinking. I'm so—"

Before he could finish, his dad smacked him hard across the face. Nick backed up again and held a hand to his face. "I'll go. I'm going."

On his way out, his dad pushed him to the ground. "Faster, boy. Maybe if you were faster, you would be playing more."

Hearing these comments almost once a week governed his drunken actions. He picked up trash and put it in their large garbage can on the side of the house. His dad stood in the yard, lighting one of his cigars. Nick didn't turn to see what he was doing. He knew from the smell that his dad was nearby. The smoky, sweet aroma is something most people wouldn't mind, but Nick loathed it. It reminded him of hatred and fear. That was when the light from the house struck the metal piece on the ground.

"Stop," said Nick's father.

Nick could tell his father had spotted it. At first, he thought he saw the axe in the yard, but no, his dad's eyes were glued on the shiny, silver *L* shape in the dirt.

"What is that? What kind of people did you have over here that would bring this?"

Nick's father picked up the gun and inspected it. Nick saw the corner of his mouth lift.

"Who brought this?"

"Let me explain—" Nick said calmly, anticipating the worst

actions from his dad.

He cut him off again, "Never mind. Just go inside. Go to bed."

"I still need to clean up."

"What did I just say? Go inside." He hit his son in the middle of his face.

Nick did as he was told and left his father holding the gun, smiling in the dim light. Only, he did not go to bed. He started packing. His head was in excruciating pain, both from the alcohol and his father's hands, but that night, he packed all the essentials, anything that could fit into his backpack and duffle bag. He decided that, of all nights, why not tonight? He had had enough of his father's cruel and utter hatred. And losing his best friend, he thought, *It's now or never*. He opened his bedroom window and left. The next morning, he would have just enough money for a bus ride to California. Hopefully, within the next few days, he would have a job and a place to stay, but it didn't matter; all that mattered was putting as much distance as possible between him and his dad.

CHAPTER TWENTY- THREE

The summer was ending, and Julian was getting ready to leave for college. He did not get into his number one choice. Ever since he stopped playing basketball, that dream vanished. He did get into a small school upstate. Watching him change the past year was hard for Beto and Maggie. He rarely picked up a basketball, his girlfriend and he separated, and he lost his relationship with his best friend and father. The attempts Beto made to talk to his son were diminished by short answers like "I have homework, Dad." Since his grades—especially in math—were the only thing he could hold on to, he got a partial scholarship to pursue a medical degree. Julian could not get over his dad's actions. It popped into his brain every time he looked at his father. The gun, he forgave; it was the days after that continued to be a splinter in his mind.

"Sheriff, I have decided to reopen the case," said Beto proudly a few days after he promised his son in the hospital.

Sheriff Castro, Bernalillo's new sheriff, sat at his desk with his mustache and beady eyes. He looked back at Beto, skeptical. He had been sheriff for a few months, though by the looks of his piles of paperwork and coffee ring-stained desk, he seemed to have been there longer.

"I know what I said the other day to your detectives, and I am not here for the gun. I am here for him because I know he is hiding for a reason."

"Who do you mean, Beto?"

It was strange to hear his first name being used that way, especially from someone he just met. *Maybe he is more informal due to his age,* Beto thought.

"Nick Walton. I want him arrested for stealing and attempting to murder my son."

"Really? Do you got any evidence?" the sheriff said, sounding more informal.

"No, and there were no witnesses, but besides me, he was the only one with a key to the bar the night I did inventory, and when I went to confront him, he was about to kill my son."

"Without more evidence or witnesses, I'm not sure what can be done."

The sheriff started to pull white papers from the large stack in front of him. After about the third or fourth paper he collected, his eyes meet Beto's. "Anything else I can do for you?"

"Oh, come on, just a search party, or take fingerprints of the bottles he swapped out to look like booze."

"Beto." He paused. "I can keep an eye out, but I have been hearing around town that he is long gone. Maybe you should let sleeping dogs lie." That came with arrogance and judgment.

Beto huffed. "Sleeping dogs lie? A real officer would wake up those damn dogs."

"Questioning the validity of my station will not help, sir."

"Who the hell elected you?" That's when Beto's anger rose.

"Well, the city. Seeing as you're so important around here, I'm surprised you didn't know that."

"Look here, son—"

"I am not your son," Castro said sharply.

"No, shit. My son would take his job seriously."

Castro waved his hand toward the back of the station as if wafting a smell toward his nose. He said louder, "Sir, I will have an officer escort you out. Thank you for coming by. As I said, I will keep a lookout."

When an officer approached, Beto bolted past him, slightly nudging him. The same officer pushed Beto out the front door of the police station. Beto waved his arms and cursed. After he screamed that he would take care of this himself, Julian walked by. There could not have been worse timing. Julian asked with a big chuckle, "What did he do now, officer?"

"Just wanted to name a suspect. I'm sure we will do our best to find him." Both Soto men could tell by the officer's tone that he was not sincere. Julian's face was a mix of shock and betrayal.

"Son, let me explain."

"You just couldn't let it go. You promised me!"

Julian walked at a brisk pace. Beto tried to keep up, but Julian was almost running.

"I needed to do it for you," Beto yelled as loud as he could.

"No, Dad." Julian turned. "This was for you. You cannot stand any injustice with this family. Your anger and distrust of anyone who is not in *the family* will be the death of you."

Both men ignored the other townspeople walking around and slowly passing by.

"What am I supposed to do? I have lost everything else."

"Add me to that list of things you have lost," Julian murmured, walking again, leaving Beto in disbelief. Standing there, he thought of two things. One: he betrayed his son's wishes and needed to do one thing he never did: apologize. Two: Sheriff Castro was not just rude or informal—he was hiding something.

CHAPTER TWENTY-FOUR

PART THREE

Twenty years later, Beto still never knew what happened to Nick or his gun. Beto had a baldhead and plenty of wrinkles. His boys were grown, and both had two sons. It took a year and multiple strong apologies, but Julian forgave him for breaking his promise. Beto went back to living his life, but with profound guilt. He imagined his dad, grandfather, and great-grandfather looking down on him with disgust. He lost their most prize possession and multiple businesses.

He thought about that night every day of his life. He was always told that the family gun would protect them, but it didn't. He often questioned what made him bring it and what would have happened if he didn't. Would Julian be dead with an axe in the head? Should he not have let his anger get to him? Nevertheless, his son got hurt and lost his dream of being a professional basketball player. Although Julian was devastated, he found another dream. Through all the pain and healing he underwent, he knew he wanted to help other people. He became a practicing doctor at the local hospital—someone who loved his work. But Beto saw something else in his eyes—sadness and regret, the notion of what could've been.

Then, the biggest question of all—*Why did I just leave it there? Something that is supposed to mean so much, and I just left it?* He guessed the sight of his son's blood squirting out like a hose was a good reason, but Beto continued to question these things almost daily. He remembered all the pain he felt when he checked the bottles at the bar and noticed the top-self bottles were not completely full. When he gathered and brought them down, he swiftly opened them. He sniffed each from the top, took a swig just in case, and found iced tea and water. His first suspect was the only one who could have done it. He remembered his son asking if he could go to a party at Nick's house that night. That was when something told Beto that he needed to go with backup. A weapon. So he raced home to get the gun before he could even think it through, not even stopping to tell Maggie. He couldn't explain the feeling, but he had a sense as if his fathers before him were whispering that something was wrong, and something definitely was. Not only did his son get hurt, but he was careless enough to forget the gun.

The same officers from the hospital looked for the gun for many years—but with no luck. They even said they could never find Nick. Beto knew Nick still had it, and wherever he was, he just hoped he kept it. He often envisioned Nick selling it or, worse, using it on someone. But his delusional thought of one day holding it again eventually faded.

Beto got home late one afternoon, and Julian was in the kitchen with his mom. Maggie was making green chile chicken enchiladas, which he could smell before he opened the front door.

"*Mijo*, what a surprise."

"Hey, Dad."

"What are you doing here so early? Where are my grandchildren?"

"At home. I decided to come alone. Sarah will bring them closer to dinner because I needed to speak with you," Julian said with a nod toward the back of the house.

The men marched into Julian's old room, which looked the same as when he was living there. His mom dusted the basketball trophies on the top shelf every week. Maggie never dared to change a thing. She decided not to redecorated so her grandchildren could stay the night.

"Dad, I found out something at the gas station today."

"Yes?"

Julian looked around the room. Part of him didn't want to tell his dad what he knew, but if his dad discovered the news another way, he would be crushed.

"I'm just gonna come right out and say it. Nick came back to town. He is living here now with his family."

Beto's eyelids opened. "That's great!"

Julian sat on his old bed. He did not expect his dad to be so happy about the news. He was more worried when he started shuffling toward the door as if in a hurry to get somewhere.

"Dad, where are you going?"

"I'm going to go pay that thief a visit. I want the gun back. I am assuming he took his dad's old place. I heard he passed away a month ago. That's where he is, isn't he?"

Julian didn't want to tell him he was right. He stayed silent. *Why couldn't he just stop and think about things before acting on them?* Julian thought. The moment he told him, he started for the door. He was concerned by his dad's actions. He wasn't angry; he was more excited than anything. *What is he going to do?* Julian pondered. He assumed his dad would go over there and kill him for taking his gun, but he was acting like he would see an old friend. He guessed the only thing he wanted was the gun back and not revenge.

Before Julian could say anything else, his dad was jiggling the keys to the still-in-good-condition Bandit.

"Wait, Dad, I am coming with you."

Just in case you need a witness, Julian thought.

CHAPTER TWENTY-FIVE

There's something about a small town—no one likes change. The house looked the same as it did the last time the Soto men were there. Julian felt an uncomfortable feeling while glancing toward the backyard.

Beto, still not showing anger, sprinted to the front door and gave a few hard knocks. By the time Julian caught up to him, a small girl, probably about five or six, answered the door. This was not who they expected. She had the same eyes and face as Nick, so Julian assumed she belonged to him.

"Where's the pizza?" she asked in a small voice.

Julian laughed. "We were wondering if your dad was home."

She nodded and ran back into the house. They couldn't see much inside, just a few moving boxes in the hallway. "Daddy," the little girl yelled. Julian and his dad heard her loud and clear even though she was in another part of the house. She said, "The pizza man has no pizza."

Nick must have said something like, "I'll go check," because before they could prepare themselves, he was standing right in front of them. He had the same pale face, with a few gray specks on a short beard and wrinkles around his eyes. His hair had a slight silver tint, but surprisingly nothing else seemed different.

The Soto men thought he would be more surprised. "I figured I would see you both sometime soon."

Beto, showing more anger, probably because Nick didn't greet them, invite them in, or beg for mercy, said, "Where's my gun?"

"I knew that's why you were here." Nick nodded multiple times.

"I swear, if you still have it, give it to me now, and you bet your sorry ass you will never have to see me again."

"Look, Mr. Soto, that night was the worst night of my life. I would never keep anything to remind me of that night."

Julian knew he was telling the truth. He never thought about how much damage that night did to Nick too. All he thought about was what it cost him. He assumed that night ruined Nick's life even more. He ran away from home and started a new life, all with the guilt hanging over him and the worry that he would eventually get caught. Julian even realized, at that moment, that he scarcely thought about that night; all he thought about was the gun. He assumed he was living fine. He had a daughter and a wife, according to the ring on his finger. He probably had a decent job, but at that moment, Julian realized he couldn't care less about Nick's life, only if he had their family heirloom, and now he knew he didn't.

Nick spoke again. "I told the police officers the same thing I'll tell you. The last time I saw the gun was on the ground. I never took it. I swear."

Beto didn't want to, but he believed him.

"What do you mean, police officers? The two officers we spoke with told us they couldn't find you."

"Well, there were definitely two of them, and they definitely found me. It was the next day, and I remember it being early, too, because I watched a few hot air balloons leaving through the sky. I was sleeping on the streets after a fight with my old man. They wanted to know absolutely every detail of the party. I was completely honest, and I told them the gun was right where I left it. Somewhere in my backyard."

Beto shouted, "Why didn't they just arrest you then and there?"

"Needed more evidence, I guess. They said they had to find the gun first, so they let me off. I always thought they were the ones who found it."

Julian turned to his father. "Why would the officers lie to us? They said they couldn't find it when they came a few days later to the hospital."

Beto didn't answer. He was still looking at Nick straight in the eyes. The whole time Nick was talking, he never blinked once, never showed nervousness. He knew it was all true. There was nothing more he could ask.

"Let's go, Son."

As the two men walked away, Nick yelled, "Hey, Julian, now that I'm back, maybe we could get together one of these days. It would be nice to catch up."

Beto was never prouder of his son than at that moment. Julian walked back toward the house, got in Nick's face, and stood his ground.

"As of today, I will never see you again. You may see me, but I will never see you. You may want to say hi when you see me at the grocery store or if our kids are in the same school play, but as far as I'm concerned, you're dead to me. I have wondered about my family's gun for almost twenty years. And now I know. As of today, I have no need for you."

Beto gave his son an accepting nod when they got in the car and pulled away from the house. They watched as the front door to Nick's house slowly shut.

"You should've punched him. That's what I would've done."

"Yes, Dad, I know you would have," Julian said with a small grin.

On the drive back, Julian felt at peace—that chapter of his life finally got an ending.

The sun was almost down, and Julian imagined the look on his mom's face when she found out what they were doing, especially since she made such a big, hot meal for dinner.

"Dad, we need to get home. Sarah and the kids should already be at your place."

"We need to make one more stop."

Julian knew exactly what his dad was planning when he yanked the steering wheel around, doing a sharp turn. He knew nothing good would happen when they pulled into the police station. Beto marched in and asked to speak to the county sheriff. Sheriff Worthington had been sheriff for three terms. People in town were starting to get tired of him. That's why he was pacing back and forth, focusing on his reelection. In a few months, he would be running against a new guy— Henry Hernandez.

"Sir, you have some men who would like to speak with you," said the receptionist that led the Soto men back to the sheriff's office.

"This late? Okay, send them in," Sheriff Worthington grumbled. He was older, with white hair, about Beto's age. He walked around his desk using a cane.

"Oh, Beto, what can I do for you?" Worthington asked pleasantly.

The sheriff and Beto had only met a few times. Once at a graduation party, the other when he came into the bar for a drink. Funny enough, both times were before he became sherriff and before Beto lost his gun. After then, Worthington seemed to keep his distance. Though that could be attributed to Beto's lack of leaving his house. Nevertheless, this was why Beto wanted to speak to him personally.

"About twenty years ago, a few officers, I believe their names were"—Beto tried to think, putting his fingers on his temple— "Morrison and some other detective, came to visit my son in the hospital after he was shot. I asked them to find the gun that shot him, and they lied and said they went to the scene and could not find it. Is any of this ringing a bell for you?"

"I am sorry, but this was way before I was sheriff. I don't know."

"You're lying." Beto noticed instantly. Looking down at him, he said, "You know where it is."

The sheriff tried to change the conversation by asking what they were doing out so late, but it was no use. Beto stood over his desk and demanded the information he needed.

"Okay, the sheriff before me, Sheriff Castro, said the gun was kept for evidence, but when you closed the case, he said it should be kept in confiscated items for good and not given back to the owner. He ordered those detectives to pretend to be on the case until it just went away. Then, I believe you reopened the investigation, but not for the gun, just for the boy."

Beto was getting more furious with every word. He could have had his gun back this entire time. He asked, "Why would he say that?"

Sheriff Worthington stood up to look Beto in the eyes. Julian stayed quiet. He knew his dad would handle this. He was usually good at getting his way—or at least he was in the past.

"All he said was to keep it confiscated. It caused too many problems. That's all I know."

Beto said the words he heard from his family. "That's not the gun's fault; it was always the person behind the gun."

The sheriff thought again. "Oh, and it was turned in. Sheriff Castro did not get it from the scene. It was turned in by someone."

"Who did that?" Julian asked.

"I'm sorry, I don't know, but I believe what Castro said. To be honest with you, you don't need a weapon. I know it, and everyone in town says that."

"Whether you believe that or not, give me what is rightfully mine, you senile man," Beto said, banging his hands on the wooden desk.

Julian butted in. "Please, sheriff, we have been without it for quiet some time. My dad just wants it back. It's a family heirloom."

"I'm sorry, boy. I know the history. I think it's best locked away. I do not feel right giving it back, and even if I wanted to, all the paperwork to get a confiscated item back would just take too much time. I need to focus on my reelection. Maybe after the election."

"You lazy, disgraceful bastard!"

Julian officially saw the highest point of his dad's anger. He had a look of disgust on his face. Julian tried to hold his father back while Beto threatened and almost attacked a police officer. An elder police officer, for that matter.

Beto ran around the desk and grabbed the sheriff by his tie, getting ready to punch his nose. He said, "I don't care how much paperwork needs to be done. You will do it, even if I have to force your hand onto every page."

"Dad, please stop!" Julian said, holding his arm back.

"Officer Hendrix," the sheriff yelled. "Please take these gentlemen out of the station. I don't want to see them in here again."

As they were escorted out in handcuffs, Beto yelled, "How dare you. You will regret this. I will end you. I am tired of people like you."

"Beto, I swear, this is why you'll never see that gun."

Julian walked steadily out of the station, trying to calm his dad, but Beto continued to fight with his arms pinned by silver handcuffs and an officer's hands.

"You're lucky I don't arrest you right now. A man in your state doesn't need a weapon like that," the sheriff yelled again while they were being pushed onto the sidewalk near the station—yet again for Beto.

CHAPTER TWENTY-SIX

Meanwhile, Sarah arrived and entered Maggie's living room. She was balancing one child on her hip and a basket of toys for her sons on the other. Both were still in the toddler stage, and she knew they needed plenty to do.

"Don't worry. I am making them cookies that will keep them busy."

"Thank you, Maggie, but they should really have dinner first."

"Honey, dessert comes before dinner at Abuela's house."

Sarah rolled her eyes. Their in-law relationship wasn't the strongest, but they got along for the most part. Sarah was blond, taller than most in the family, and had much lighter skin. Safe to say, she kind of stuck out. It also didn't help that she was only fluent in English, so when Maggie started conversations in Spanish, it enhanced the feeling of being an outcast. She tried her hardest to pick up the language, but it never stuck.

Maggie gave a full plate of chocolate chip cookies and a glass of milk to her grandsons. They sat and watched cartoons on the TV.

"Only for a few minutes, boys," Sarah said.

"Oh, so many rules. These children are perfect just the way they are."

"I know. It's just that I read that we should be limiting time in front of the TV."

"You do tend to read a lot of these parenting books, don't you? Have you had any thoughts about going back to work?"

That hit a sore spot for Sarah. She had a good job in marketing but decided to be a stay-at-home mom. She never thought that would happen, but Julian made enough to support the family.

"I will. I am waiting a few more years until both boys are in school."

"I know, sweetie. I didn't mean anything by it. I was a stay-at-home mom my whole life, and look how good I turned out," Maggie said with a chuckle.

Sarah sighed with a forced smile. She checked the wall clock and wondered what was taking Julian so long. The conversation between her and Maggie was getting awkward and almost painful. It wasn't until she asked how Julian was doing that Sarah started to open up.

"Oh, well, I don't know. Ever since he found that guy from high school they went to see, he has seemed kind of obsessed with the past."

"Really? I always thought he stayed away from all that family drama. I found him to be more like his aunt. You know, kind of calmer and doesn't care much about all that history."

Sarah was shocked that Maggie didn't notice how much it bothered him. She knew from the moment she met Julian in college that he was a mama's boy, so she was surprised she didn't know how upset he was about Nick's return.

"Yeah, he has been. I just worry it's all getting to him."

"What do you mean?"

"Oh, you know, just living in the past can make you angry. I just don't want to see him turn out—" *What am I saying?* Sarah thought as she stopped herself. *Do I not realize who I am talking to?*

"What, like his dad?" Maggie said, looking her straight in the eyes.

"I don't mean it to sound like that."

Maggie adjusted in her seat. She seemed to pause for a long moment. The only sound was *Blue's Clues* on the TV.

"I know what they say about him, and he isn't the friendliest guy in town, but I knew that going into our marriage. I know the man he really is, and that is the man he is with me."

"I know. I apologize. I just don't see Julian as the angry type, and these past few days, he has seemed to be going in that direction."

"Julian isn't like that. Now, his brother, maybe, but no, not Julian, and I'm not just saying that. You know the type of person he is. That is why I know how good you are for my son."

Sarah's eyes widened. *An approval from Maggie?* It was a compliment. They were bonding. Maggie told a story that made Sarah look at her and her marriage in a new way.

"Can I tell you something, Sarah? I have never told anyone. Just Elizabeth and I know."

Sarah gave a gentle smile. "Yes, of course. Elizabeth, your friend down the street, right?"

"Yes. When Julian and Edward were little, Elizabeth was married to a horrible man. He was emotionally and physically abusive. I don't even remember his name; he was *awful*."

Sarah looked confused but she let Maggie finish.

"Well, she would not confide in anyone else. I told her time and again to leave him or tell the police, but she begged me not to, and she especially did not want Beto knowing. Can you imagine what he would do?"

Sarah nodded her head, wanting the story to continue. "So, what happened? Because I know she is not married anymore."

"Well, Beto did, in fact, find out. One day, she came over, and Beto could tell she was hurt. She had bruises on her arms and tears in her eyes. When he questioned her, she tried to cover up for him but couldn't." Maggie paused to catch her breath. "Beto went straight over to their house, but her husband was not there. He stepped out, lucky for him. Elizabeth promised Beto and I that that was it. That night, she would leave him and stay with us."

"Let me guess. She didn't?"

"No, and when Beto was going to go over there again, I asked him not to. I made him promise he wouldn't. I said I would take care of it."

"So, what did you do?" Sarah asked, acting as if she was watching a telenovela.

"I was furious. Furious at the both of them, but I took it out on him. I marched into their house one day when I knew Elizabeth was out buying groceries. I found her husband eating in the kitchen. I had met him before, but he was terrified to see me breaking into their house in such a rage, oh, and holding the revolver."

"You brought a gun?"

"Of course. I wanted to scare the hell out of him. I raised it up and told him never to touch her again. Whether she stays with him or not, he will never touch her like that again."

Maggie stopped, and Sarah thought that was it. She couldn't imagine little Maggie Soto holding a gun to someone and threatening them.

"So, she left him?"

"Well, yes, but only after I told her that he tried to hurt me too."

"What!" Sarah yelled, providing more expression on her face and in that house than ever before. The boys peeled their eyes from the spotted blue dog. When they noticed it wasn't as exciting as they thought, and in a synchronous motion, they both turned back to the TV.

"After he calmed down from the initial sight of me, he giggled and pushed me, trying to reach for the gun. While getting my footing, he punched me right here." She pointed above her belly button. "He said, 'You don't think I have one of those too?' I pulled myself up, the gun steady in one hand, and said a phrase that made him stop dead in his tracks."

In complete shock, Sarah asked, "What did you say?"

"I said, 'You might, but we all know I can get away with it.' After that, he yelled at me to get out of his house, which I did, but slowly and with pride.

"Woah, I can't believe you did that. You're a badass, Maggie."

Maggie smiled and said, "Next to every Soto man is an even stronger woman willing to do the same for her family."

The men pulled up in the driveway much later than they said. Sarah wondered again what took so long. As the car turned off, Sarah asked, "Maggie, can I be honest with you?"

"Of course."

"There's always been a rumor around town about abusive marriages."

Maggie squinted her eyes and nodded as if she knew what Sarah was about to say.

"Well," she said quickly, "everyone thought it was your marriage."

Maggie laughed. "I do love this town. I don't mind the rumors anymore. I find them rather entertaining."

CHAPTER TWENTY-SEVEN

A few days passed, and it seemed that Beto's anger decreased. Julian was still cautious around his dad. They knew that having the gun again was impossible, but there were many gaps in the story that the Soto men desperately wanted to solve. There was one person who could answer these questions, but where could Julian find him? He wondered if he was even still alive.

He asked around town. There was usually one or two older ladies who knew everything about everyone. One thing was certain—he needed to do this alone. It seemed every time his dad got involved, it made things worse. He pictured it in his mind—his dad being thrown out of the police station for a third time. Or even worse, his dad being locked up.

After ringing doors and asking some older folks at the nearby diner, he got his answer.

"Why are you looking for him?"

"I was just wondering what happened after he lost the election to Worthington."

One lady, Cynthia, said, "Well, people believe he gave up the election. He was tired of the job, which was strange, especially because he was so young at the time."

"Castro, you all are talking about," a gentleman in jeaned suspenders chimed in. "Our youngest head sheriff ever, I believe. He went to the city. He's taking care of his elderly aunt."

"That's right," Cynthia said. "She is the only family he had left. I met her once. I remember very little. I bet I can tell you the part of town she lives in, but I don't know specifics."

"That's fine. Anything would help," Julian said.

His search continued around town. He received more information, but nothing too helpful. Cynthia told him to get in contact with Laura on First Street. She said that lady takes notes on the town as a hobby. Julian didn't believe her, but he should have. After ringing the doorbell, an almost ninety-year-old lady invited him in with pleasure. *Anything for a gossip session*, Julian assumed. They sat at her kitchen table that was covered with round lilac doilies.

"Like I said, I am trying to get in contact with him. I believe he is staying at his aunt's house or at least taking care of her."

"Why do you want to speak to him?" Laura's eyes narrowed, and she folded her short, white hair behind her good ear. She reached into the cabinet drawer behind her chair. Julian knew she had the answer, but she wasn't going to provide it without information in return.

He imagined her writing down this conversation when he left. "Oh, my dad wanted to give him something that he found."

"Really? Like what?"

"Just an, um, old photo of him. For some reason, my mother took the photo during his service, and they would like him to have it."

Her frail hand unfolded. "Can I see this photo?"

"Oh, I left it at my dad's. Wanted to keep it safe."

She squinted her eyes. After situating her oversized glasses, she flipped through her notebook. Julian was too far to see what was written, just scribbles in various colors.

"Nope, not this book," she mumbled to herself.

This lady needs another hobby, Julian thought. In the third journal, she found an address. She slid the journal across the table so Julian could copy the address into his pocket notebook.

"Oh, yes, I remember talking to his aunt after her family left. It was quite a shock to learn she was his aunt. She used to live in this town. I'm surprised you didn't know that."

Julian wondered why she thought he would know when he didn't take notes on everyone like she did. He thanked her and created a plan to go the very next day.

On his hour-long drive, he practiced his speech and questions. He pictured Castro shutting the door in his face.

He arrived at the small, probably two-bedroom, house on the west side of the city. He pressed the round doorbell. Nothing. So, he did it again. Before the third time, the door was opened by an older Sheriff Castro. The full mustache was still there, though it had turned a peppered gray. He was probably eight or nine years younger than Beto but much taller. He had the same light eyes and dark skin.

"How can I help you?" Castro asked, keeping the door slightly closed.

"Sherriff Castro?"

"Well, yeah, who are you?"

"My name is Julian. I have a few questions I wanted to ask you. It won't take long."

He slowly opened the door. "Ask me about what?"

"Well, about something that, um . . . something that you, you see, well," Julian mumbled and turned red. *So much for the practice*, he thought.

"What did you say your name was?"

"Julian. Julian Soto."

Castro's eyes enlarged as he pushed the door wide open. "Please come in, boy."

"Thank you," Julian said with a surprising tone. "That's very nice. It won't take long."

"Anything for Beto's son, right?" Julian nodded. Castro asked him to sit at the small table in the kitchen. The house was fairly clean but with a musty smell. Castro rushed to the back of the house. Julian wondered what he needed before their conversation.

"Just needed to inform my aunt we have a visitor. She hasn't been too well. So, what did you need from me?" Castro asked while taking a seat at the table.

"Well, you were working when I was in high school, and there was this kid, Nick Walton. Anyway, he's back in town. I got some information from him and wanted to know if it's true."

"That was a while back. I'm not sure I can help or remember," he said with a chuckle.

"Right, I understand, but if anything rings a bell, let me know. Since he was back, we wanted to know what happened to the revolver my father brought and left at his house the night of his end-of-the-school-year party."

"And what did he say?"

"He said he never picked it up. He remembered seeing it in his backyard. Well, my father and I believe him."

"And"—Castro crossed his arms and paused—"what do you need me for?"

"Your officers at the time told us they could not find it either."

Then again, with even more aggression, he said, "Yeah, so?"

"Well, sir, I'm here to ask how you somehow got the item and confiscated it. We know it is still confiscated today."

Castro's smile widened. "Look at the Sherlocks over here."

"I'm asking for the truth. We know we won't see it again, but I need to know what happened."

He paused, leaned back in his chair, and said, "I'm going to tell you a story, boy, one I haven't told too many people. Well, because they probably wouldn't even believe me."

Julian settled in his chair.

"My father was a hardworking man. He came from absolutely

nothing. People say that all the time. 'My ancestors came from nothing,' but my father really had nothing. He lived in a one-bedroom home with his family and slept on blankets, no bed. Even after he moved and worked tirelessly, he came back home with nothing. Just one dollar bill to his name. He had job after job. He worked for rich men who treated him poorly, gave him a few cents, and booted him out."

Julian wondered what this had to do with his question. He even gave an understanding nod, but he was completely confused.

Castro continued, "Everyone around him, friends and people in his town, thought he was some sort of rebel. They thought he was uncommitted or lazy, but I know it was neither. He was a good, hardworking man who, unfortunately, died too soon in his middle age."

Castro paused, looking at Julian, waiting for him to interject, but Julian was hesitant. He could tell that Castro was once a politician. His story was intriguing and clearly stated, rehearsed, even.

"Well, after he got back into town, he asked one of his friends for money, just to get him by until he found a job in town. This friend and his family, let's call them the Snakes, had it all. They were loaded, but greedy. It was the same time as the Great Depression, and they had plenty to give, but they never helped those outside their own snakeskin. So, he said no and brushed my father off. A few days later, the Snakes' home was broken into, and their family jewelry was taken. Who do you think they all suspected?"

Julian sat up. *Why is this starting to sound strange?* he thought. *Not strange, almost familiar.* He needed more information, so he jumped in. "Well, did they talk to your father?"

"My father was asked out to the desert one night for a party, and no, his friend didn't just talk to him, that Snake threatened him with a gun to his head. My father pleaded with him and begged him to believe it wasn't him. So, he had a choice, either fight his way out of the situation or end up dead. My father fought the Snake and won. Everyone in town believed that my father shot the gun, but it was him; it was the own Snake that accidentally shot himself."

"Sir, I am not sure you heard this story correctly."

"Same old Sotos, trying to cover up their own mistakes, always looking out for their own. Greedy bastards."

"So, let me get this straight. What you're saying is your father is—"

"Yes," Castro cut him off. "My father was Ruben Valdez."

CHAPTER TWENTY-EIGHT

Julian put a hand to his forehead. "How is this even possible?" He tried to do the math, and it was somewhat adding up. The years were stretched a bit, but it could be true.

"What?" Castro said louder, "Your family always just ended the story there, huh? They never thought to see what actually happened to old Ruben?"

"He went to jail for life. He, well, he died in jail. At least that is what everyone thought."

"Oh, of course they did. Well, now that I have you, and now that you know the real story, let me tell you how it ended. After seven years of telling his inmates and guards the true story, one guard felt horrible for him. He knew my father was telling the truth and that he'd never get out, so he let him out. Multiple guards got on board and devised a plan to say the inmate died in his cell. My father walked all the way to the nearest town. Facing off wildlife and no food or water for days, he made it to Santa Fe. There, he worked as a cook in a local restaurant."

"You're telling me that after seven years in prison for killing my dad's uncle, he moved to the town forty-five minutes away?"

Castro slammed both hands on the table and yelled, "He did not kill anyone."

"Okay, if he didn't, why did he stay in a town so close to where he could be recognized?"

"Because that is where I was."

He briefly paused to look at a picture on the wall. It was blurry, but Julian assumed the small, brunette woman must have been his mother, who wasn't around anymore, either.

"My mother was a waitress in that restaurant. She was much younger, but she fell for him. He told her everything about his past— why he couldn't leave his apartment much and never used his real name. Robin Valenzuela. Same initials, so it was easier to remember the alias."

"Why didn't all three of you move away?"

"After a while, he noticed that people didn't care. No one was looking for Ruben Valdez. Everyone assumed he died. So, for the last decade of his life, he lived a free man."

So many questions cluttered Julian's mind, "Why do you go by Castro?"

"It was my mother's last name. They never married; you can probably guess why. My father died of cancer when I was nine, and then my mother died when I was right out of college."

Julian was silent, taking it all in. He considered the great loss Castro had gone through—to not only lose one parent but two at such early ages. How fortunate he was to still have both his parents. He wanted to jump in with condolences, but all he could think of was Ruben Valdez. How was this possible? How was Ruben Valdez right under their noses for years? He pictured what his grandfather or great-grandfather would have done if they had known someone who stole, lied, and betrayed their family was one town over. Whatever story he conjured up for his own guilty heart was disgraceful. Julian had many more questions, but he could tell Castro got what he wanted. It was almost as if Julian's visit was the best thing that could've happened to him. He wanted to tell his story to what he calls a Snake.

"If you believe this, why didn't you tell people? Why didn't you ask my dad about it?"

"After I was elected, I started with a few people, but this town is so wrapped around your family's finger, it wasn't worth the breath. Most people ignored it or laughed it off."

"So, that's why you ran for county sheriff?" Julian asked, piecing the puzzle together.

"I wanted everyone to see how unfair it is to live in a small town with a family like yours. You people had everything and never shared it. There should never be a king in a small town."

"Well, I guess you got what you wanted."

"It was about time. My term was coming to an end, and everything was getting better. Bigger stores were coming to town, the population was going up, and the family-run businesses weren't making it. All the smaller businesses were dying, as they should. Who do you think helped the mayor bring that little town into the twenty-first century?"

"And that's why you weren't upset about the election against Worthington? You got what you wanted."

"The family that took so much from my father was finally getting what they deserved."

Julian's heart raced. His entire life, he wondered why he didn't have the Soto temper, and maybe it was because of this. The Soto men would kill Castro right then and there. Maybe it was for the best that he came to talk to him alone. "Well, I want you to know we are still standing."

"Of course you all are, but I got what I needed."

"You're talking about the gun?"

Castro had a sinister smile under his mustache.

"Why didn't you just keep it for yourself?"

"You all would have found out eventually and hunted me down. This way, it is locked away forever. My own sense of justice. The next sheriff agreed that I was right too." Castro leaned back with his hands on his head. "Are we done now?"

"Last question. How did you even get your hands on it?"

"Your friend, Walton, right? His father brought it in early that next morning. The moment I saw it, it was like hearing my father's story all over again. Everything fell into place. It was the last thing I could take as revenge, especially since no one knew the real story of that night."

Julian was fuming. He remembered Nick's sleazy father. Why would he turn it in? He needed one last question, but Castro got up and led him to the door.

"Why would Nick's father just hand it over?" Julian asked, following him.

"Oh, I had to pay him a couple hundred, but it was worth every penny."

Julian's face grew red, and he had to say something before he left. "You are a disgrace. You plotted this for years for nothing. You have it all wrong." Julian yelled louder than ever, "How could you even believe such crap?"

"Goodbye, Julian. Wonderful visiting with you," Castro said as he pushed him out and shut the door, leaving Julian to hear the faint laughter of a bitter, jealous man.

Although Julian's head was spinning, he drove straight to his father's house, ready to tell him everything, but once there, he sat in the driveway for far too long. He wrestled with the idea of telling his father what he had discovered. He knew there were various stories of his family's past, but he had never heard that one. He thought his dad had the right to know, especially since losing the grocery store and orchards was not entirely the "future's fault." Beto had always blamed the closing businesses on the changing world, and while that was somewhat true, knowing more about Castro's role behind those losses might help his dad. He could see how hard that was on his father.

Julian recalled a time toward the end when he walked into the store, and it was empty. The shelves of produce and fresh foods were almost gone. His dad was working behind one of the registers since they could not afford to keep employees.

"Dad, you have to get more supplies. No one is coming because the shelves are bare."

His dad walked out from behind the register. "We have tried that, *mijo*. I've kept everything stocked for months, then had to throw out pounds of brown, soggy lettuce and spoiled milk because no one was here."

"Well, there must be something else we can try. We can—"

Beto cut him off and yelled, "Julian, we have tried everything. You would know that if you came to help out more instead of playing basketball all the damn time."

With that memory in mind and everything that just happened at the sheriff's office, he decided to wait a while, and by a while, he meant maybe even years.

He knew it was the right decision. Every action, whether good or bad, had always been spur-of-the-moment for his father. Julian knew his actions were never backed by logic. He thought back to the senior party and his dad bringing the gun, then arriving at the police station after his promise, and then showing up at Nick's the minute after finding out he was back in town. There was never patience when it came to his dad. There was no way this would end up well if Julian busted in there and told him his new discoveries. He sat in the car and pictured his father learning about Castro's version and driving straight over there to threaten him or beat him up. Though that would look rather ironic since Castro was younger, taller, and most likely stronger than his dad. Julian decided it's best to let the story end before revealing the twist.

When he walked inside his family's home, it was like he was seeing things for the first time. He saw his dad and sat next to him on the sofa. Beto questioned why he was there.

"I just wanted to come by and say hi."

Beto knew his son's expressions and knew that was a lie. Julian always had an easy tell. Whether it was a slight nose wrinkle or no eye contact, it was never difficult to tell when he knew something. Beto surprisingly let it go and hoped he would learn about it soon.

CHAPTER TWENTY-NINE

When Beto realized that Henry Hernanadez would be his last hope at not letting down his family, he took it, though he wasn't going to lie to Henry. He was honest. He did want to shoot someone—anyone who had done him wrong—and Sheriff Worthington was first on his list.

After admitting to the future sheriff that he needed to commit a murder, Beto worried if he would ever see that gun again. Maybe Sheriff Worthington was right. Maybe he took this too far and didn't deserve to have the gun back in his state of mind. That thought passed like lightning when he found out through the nightly news that Henry was elected for sheriff. He held up his side of the deal. He talked to neighbors and friends. He discussed his support for Henry, which was surprisingly genuine. Most everyone agreed with his vote, especially since Worthington was much older. He knew this plan was his last hope. If he didn't get his gun back, he would leave it alone. Beto noticed how angry he got at the former sheriff and admitted to the new one that he was going to use the gun on someone; it was just stupid. That wasn't the kind of man he wanted to be, but it was the one he had been in the past.

Of all the things he wanted to do, he knew what he needed to do first. He found Maggie in the bedroom and asked her to sit on the bed. He pulled up a chair to face her.

"I know I have a problem," Beto said while moving his chin closer to his chest.

"Oh, you just now realize it. I keep telling you to throw your dirty clothes in the hamper," she said with a chuckle.

"No, I mean, yes, I can work on that too, but what I need to work on is inside me." Beto placed his fingers on his chest. "I don't know why I lose it sometimes, even over small things."

Maggie took his hands in hers. She hoped this realization would happen someday.

Beto said, "I don't know how you have watched it over the past years, barely saying anything. I just wish I was more like Denny. She couldn't care less about this family stuff."

"It is always different being the eldest sibling, but, *mi amor*, I know you. I knew the man you were before we were married." Maggie patted his callused hands.

"I want to do better. I know some things in the past did not warrant that much anger."

Maggie tilted her head and raised an eyebrow.

"Okay, *most* of those times, but I'm saying thank you. I'm giving up this past nonsense."

She noticed he was almost in tears. He lowered his head, and she gave him a kiss on the forehead. So many years have gone by, and so much hurt has happened to him; she knew that anger was bound to rise, but she hardly pictured him realizing or even apologizing. It was like watching a balloon deflate. She thought back to her conversation with Sarah.

"It's like I told Sarah the other day. Next to every Soto man is an even stronger woman willing to do the same." She smiled. "Just maybe not in the same style as you would, but it's because of your past and these stories that make you so passionate about your family."

Beto would no longer pursue this hopeless dream; it only led him down a useless road. He decided to leave it up to Henry. If he wanted to help out Beto, especially since Beto told half the town to vote for him, then that would be up to him. Beto decided to put it to fate.

Fate worked out well for him, but not instantly. A month passed before Henry called Beto and asked him to come to the station. He knew Beto would not be welcome because of the incident three months earlier, so he said to come after dark.

When that night came, Beto could barely hold it together. He figured he would be seeing the gun that night. Like meeting a long lost relative or welcoming home a soldier who had been away at war, the excitement was consuming every thought. Beto showed up with excitement but also fear. *What if this meeting is for something else?* Beto pondered. *What if it is just to thank me for the election and not to reward me?* After multiple attempts of not getting what he wanted in that building, he suddenly expected not to receive the gun.

Henry stood tall and proud of his new position. He went straight to the point. "We had a deal. Thank you for helping me get elected. I want to do this right, so I am going to leave my office. It's in my desk." Henry threw him a key. "Lock my door when you're done."

Beto's hand was shaking, but he opened the drawer with the key after Henry left. Staring up at him was his great-grandfather's silver gun with the initials G.S. It had been a long time. The gun was supposed to be used only for protection, but it had caused more pain. Still, he was relieved to have it. Finally, his family heirloom that he would never lose. Never again.

Beto slid the gun into his jacket pocket and shut the drawer. He locked up and walked out of the office. As he passed Henry in the front of the station, Henry said, "Beto, I have to ask you to be reasonable. I don't want you to hurt someone or get yourself in trouble."

Beto smiled. "Would you like to come to my house soon? I'd like to tell you my story."

Henry was surprised and accepted the offer. The two men sat at the Soto's kitchen table that next week. It was late, and Maggie was already in bed. Beto poured them both a glass of whiskey.

That's when Henry Hernandez heard the entire Soto family story. Since he didn't grow up in the small town of Bernalillo, he had never heard the tale. So, Beto told him everything. He talked about his family's immigration from Spain, his family businesses, his uncle's death, his son's triumph over a former friend, and even his own mistakes. The story came out fluidly as if he was telling his grandkids or great-grandkids, hoping they would pass it on one day.

Henry paused for a long time. Then he nodded. "I see now the true reason you wanted the gun back."

"Henry, I like you, and I truly agree that you were the best candidate. That's why I told people to vote for you, not because of the gun. I wasn't going to bother you about it again. I saw what not having it was doing to me. I may not have much longer on this earth, but I want to make sure I leave it as a better man."

Henry looked perplexed. "So, do you not want it anymore?"

"*Sí*, I do, but not for the reason I told you."

Henry tilted his head with an inquisitive look.

Beto sighed. "I told you that out of anger. And to be honest, I really did want to shoot someone. Worthington was top on my list, especially because he refused to give me the gun, but I wanted to kill more than just him. I wanted revenge on every person who had ever touched the gun and tried to hurt my family."

Henry nodded sincerely.

"Many people have tried to take the gun or use it when they were not supposed to. I admit . . . I have been one of those people at times," Beto said with remorse.

"So, maybe you should just get rid of it?"

"I would, but that's not what my dad would have wanted or his dad, for that matter. I am going to pass it down like it is supposed to be, but not right away. I have a feeling wherever it goes, it will cause more harm than good. So, it will be a while. Maybe my kids or grandkids will want it someday because it is rightfully theirs. It stays in the family."

Henry said, "Guns are easier to get nowadays. Why do you think they will want it?"

Beto smiled half-heartedly. "The same reason I want it. It is not about having it as a weapon. It's about having something from the past. I could have gotten a replacement, but it never seemed right. Almost disgraceful. I have lost so much given to me by my family. It's one piece of this town I am glad to have back."

The men talked until almost midnight. He thanked Beto for having him over and being so honest. He wondered what his next steps would be, but he knew that whatever Beto did would be in his family's best interest. He seemed to be in a better mindset—as if the gun made him at peace.

CHAPTER THIRTY

One day later, Beto opened the bar in the early morning. The sun broke through the dark room. No one was there, and he locked the door behind him, just in case someone saw him and wanted to pop in. He entered his office and did the same to the office door.

He opened his jacket pocket and pulled out the Colt 45 revolver. Everyone in town, including his family and sister, thought the valuables were in the bank. Beto liked it this way. He felt better knowing their money was somewhere he went often. Although he never opened the safe, he could still keep his eye on it. Only Maggie and Beto knew the true location. They never shared this secret, not even with their sons.

Beto walked over to the painting of the Rio Grande and slid it over to reveal the safe. He tried not to disturb the thin layer of dust, to make it look like he was never there, then turned the dial. He was the only one who knew the combination—a code only he would be clever enough to come up with. It was easy to remember, especially as he aged.

He opened the safe and pushed the black door back. There he

stood for a few moments, almost taking inventory. He looked at multiple bars of gold and silver, about a hundred stacks of cash, and another hundred rolls of coins. There were deeds to their land and a few pieces of jewelry. Some were pieces that George's mom had left. He found a place for the gun, sitting on top of a hundred years of the family's hard work.

He felt better. A few weeks ago, anger and resentment consumed him. Now, he accomplished something. Although he lost almost everything his family built, at least he got the revolver back, and he still had something in the safe. He could have used that wealth throughout the years, but he pretended it wasn't there. Looking at the weapon on top of their fortune, he felt relaxed, knowing the heirloom was in a good place. Before barely closing the safe, he noticed someone behind him. It was more than just one person. He pictured his family looking at him, all standing in the office together.

There was his dad with his stern facial expression and his mom with her heart on her sleeve and a scrunched tissue in her hand. Next to them was George with his handsome face and goofy smile. Then, his grandparents, Lorenzo and Mary, smaller and older, but still very happy. Finally, the original owner, in suspenders and a mustache—the cowboy, George Soto. Beto pictured him speaking in a gravelly voice and telling the story again, about how proud his parents would be, especially coming from Spain with no shoes and one coin in each hand. Beto laughed, knowing how much that had changed over the years. Not just the story, but their family.

More than anything, he hoped he didn't let them down. At least he saved the gun, which had been held and used by so many in this very room, which might be held and used by so many more. He thought about each one and what they had gone through. He had heard their stories so many times. Beto now understood that it was the stories of the past that influenced the future. That's the thing about heritage—unless you have lived it, all you can go off of is what you have been told. Whether it was how they immigrated from Spain, how his uncle died, or even how he lost and gained that gun back, it was his family's stories that he holds on to. It is these stories that make him the man he is. He hoped this ending made them all proud.

Beto glanced around the room again, and they were gone. He, especially out of everyone in their family, knew they were nowhere near perfect, but they always tried to put family first. Beto had a rare smile on his face. One that showed acceptance. He shut the safe and twisted the dial with hopes that its door would not be opened anytime soon.

THE END

THE SOTO FAMILY TREE

GEORGE SOTO
& ANNE SOTO

LORENZO SOTO
& MARY SOTO

BERNARD SOTO
& SUSAN SOTO

GEORGE SOTO

BERNARD "BETO" SOTO JR.
& MAGGIE SOTO

DENNY SOTO

EDWARD SOTO

JULIAN SOTO
& SARAH SOTO

END NOTE

To learn more about the Silva family (referred to as the Soto family in the book), please read the following and listen to *El Corrido de George Silva*.

https://digitalrepository.unm.edu/shri_publications/57/

Printed in the USA
CPSIA information can be obtained
at www.ICGtesting.com
JSHW020031280424
61932JS00004B/169